CHOSEN

THE IMMORTAL ONES - BOOK ONE

Shade Owens

PROLOGUE

rack.

My head rocked back and forth, and my surroundings blurred. Was my jaw unhinged? And what was that rusty smell? Blood?

I opened my mouth wide until a loud popping sound echoed in my ears.

Why was everything so fuzzy? How hard had he hit me?

I blinked hard, trying to clear the haze.

Suddenly, the man grabbed me from behind and my heart skipped a beat. My heels scraped the floor as he dragged me through a series of doors.

"No!" I wanted to shout, but I was too disoriented.

Instead, I reached everywhere I could, clawing the air as I tried to latch onto something solid enough to stop this man from dragging me. But I was too weak. Everything I touched slipped away.

"Since you want to be a hero," he growled, "you can go next."

Although I couldn't see his face, the way he spoke made it sound like he was smiling.

He was enjoying this.

When the door next to me blasted open and a powerful gust of wind blew in, I knew exactly what was about to happen—I was going to die.

CHAPTER 1

They spoke about Selection Day as if it were like winning a large sum of money—whatever *money* was. I'd read about it but didn't quite understand it. Grandma told me that in the old days, people used something called *money* to spend however they liked. She explained that this *money* could be exchanged for food, toys, clothing, and even vehicles.

I hadn't understood what a vehicle was, so she explained it to me, too. Something about a metal frame on wheels, like a horse chariot, only it was run on oil and gas. It sounded like science fiction to me, like something that could only exist in the future, not the past.

And how was it even possible to buy belongings? To own property?

Freedom, Grandma had called it. I always wondered what that kind of freedom felt like.

Some days, I fantasized about walking into

something Grandma referred to as a grocery store. She'd described it as brightly lit and full of vibrant fruits and vegetables. The more she spoke about the past, the more I wanted to travel in time like the characters in an old book I kept hidden under my bed—*The Time Machine* by H. G. Wells.

"I need it more!" Grunwalt said, leaning back in his wooden chair and smoothing the wrinkles on his face. "Ya see these? Ain't no goin' back from this."

Poor Grunwalt. I felt sorry for him. Not because he was old and grumpy, but because every time he talked about his life, it sounded empty. No partner, no children, no friends... His entire existence, or at least what he talked about, had revolved around him trying to get a dose of the Ambrosia Serum.

Kiatha sat next to him. She leaned forward until her dark elbows formed indents in her thighs. She smiled, the light of the fire making her brown skin look creamier than usual. "What I wouldn't do to feel thirty again."

Kiatha was in her midforties. But like everyone else in Division 9, all she ever spoke about was Selection Day. I didn't blame her or the others. Everyone wanted to be selected to join the Elites.

We couldn't go back in time, but we could join the Elites. That was everyone's dream.

That was the reason people worked so hard all year long: to earn a chance at a life that was said to be eternal bliss.

To be ageless.

To be immortal.

To live like royalty and never want for anything.

"Thirty years I been waitin' for this," Grunwalt said. "It's finally our turn. It's gotta be."

By turn, he meant Division 9's turn at being selected to take part in the lottery. Every year, the Elites chose one division from all of Lutum, and from this division, they selected a single person. The odds of being selected were roughly 1:2000, which according to Grandma, were great odds.

"You don't want to be a Producer your entire life, do you?" Grandma would often say to me.

It was like she'd given up on the idea of eternal youth and only wanted the best for me. And now that I was seventeen, winning the lottery was a real possibility.

Did I want to leave Division 9? Yes, but not by joining human beings capable of making countless others suffer so they could live comfortable lives. Every evening, Producers from within our section gathered around a fire and spoke of joining the Elites like it was the same thing as receiving a gift from the gods.

I'd always wondered why the Elites couldn't share their serum with everyone. According to Grandma, more than 98 percent of the world's population was wiped out during the war—a war caused by the serum... chaos caused by human beings wanting to live forever, but not having the means to afford the serum. But now, with only 2 percent of the world's population remaining, why keep it from us? Why not let everyone live in abundance? It didn't make sense.

Closing my eyes, I pictured Grandma's face from the day before. She'd been hunched over with a rounded back, working hard in the gardens. When she sensed me approach, she pulled her face out from the bushes, a thin layer of dirt coating her veiny, bulbous nose. "It's all for control, Silverstasia."

Grandma was the only one who ever called me by my full name. Everyone else called me Silver.

"How would they survive without us?" she said. With a muddy finger, she tapped her translucent temple next to her salt-and-pepper hair. "Think about it. We're basically slaves. If we were all ageless and immortal, we wouldn't care about anything. We wouldn't feel the need to work our butts off to gain points every year."

Grandma was right. In every division, Producers were awarded points for good behavior and strong production. After every lottery, the score was wiped clean and we started over again. Both divisions and Producers were selected to take part in the draw based on their points. No one understood it, but some speculated that if you fell within a certain range of points, you were included in the draw.

So only the top-producing divisions in all of Lutum were placed in the lottery, and once a single division was selected, only the top producers from that division were placed in the lottery. This meant everyone was always on their best behavior.

Mother's footsteps echoed behind us, shaking me out of my daydream.

"You all know the serum doesn't reverse aging," she said, her tone bitter. Although I refused to look up at her, I sensed her eyes narrow on me. "Now quit your dreamin' 'n get to bed before the Defenders get involved."

Without a word, Grunwalt stood, picked up a bucket of dirty water, and spilled it over the fire.

CHAPTER 2

on't mind your mother," Grandma said. She swept my hair over my shoulders and let it fall behind my back. With a twinkle in her eye, she pulled a bright red elastic from her pocket. "For luck."

"Where'd you find that?" I asked.

Bright colors were forbidden in Lutum... something about heightened emotions. Everyone was given the same clothes: beige hemp suits that turned brown after a few days of work.

The worst part? These clothes weren't even provided by the Elites. They were sewn internally by Samara, our seamstress.

"What makes you think I'm even in the lottery this year?" I asked.

I was only a farmer; I helped Grandma with her chores, and that was it. How could I have possibly earned enough points to be in the lottery? Without a word, she moved behind me and smiled, making a wet clicking sound.

"Whether it's today or another day, sweetheart, you *will* make it to Olympus."

I'd always thought the name *Olympus* sounded funny. It wasn't until Grandma explained Greek mythology to me that I understood why the Elites had picked such a unique name. They thought of themselves as gods.

"What if I don't want to be in Olympus?" I asked.

Her grip tightened around my ponytail. "I won't let you turn out like your mother."

Mother was cold and distant. The last thing I wanted was to end up like her. Ever since I was a child, Mother had been this way. It was like she hated me, and I'd never understood why. Swallowing hard, I stared at my bare feet.

We sat in silence for what felt like hours as Grandma prepared me for Selection Day. With a sponge soaked with cold water, she wiped mud off my cheeks and hands and from underneath my fingernails. Then, she reached for something underneath a tuft of grass and extracted a purple flower.

My eyes popped. "Where'd you find that?"

Flowers, due to their vibrant colors, were also forbidden in Lutum.

"I've been growing a garden of flowers in secret," she said, placing a finger over my lips.

"Grandma—" I tried, but she wouldn't listen.

Why would she do something like that? If she got caught—

"Here," she said, dabbing the flower against my neck. "To smell clean."

I breathed in deep, salivating over the floral scent.

Then, she scrunched the flower with its leaves and tucked it inside my pocket. "Also for good luck."

I smiled. "You're very... What's that word again?" I asked.

"Superstitious," she said, tapping the tip of my nose as if I were a five-year-old child.

Her large, hazel eyes narrowed on me. "Are you still reading every night?"

I nodded. "I do, but Mother says Producers should spend more time resting than reading."

The truth was, Mother had thrown many of my books into the fire, but I didn't bring it up. Grandma already didn't like Mother, and as cold as Mother was with me, I didn't want to get her in trouble.

Grandma frowned, the folds on her face deepening. "I swear, that batshit crazy woman—"

I chuckled. Grandma always talked funny. She spoke in slang and used words that most Producers would likely never hear in their lifetime. Where did she come up with these things? Were they words people had once used in the Old World?

"I have a secret stash under my bed," she said. "Every evening before supper, while your mother's busy preparing the meal, I want you to pick up a book and read, okay? Don't let anyone see you. Sit quietly and read."

I nodded.

Ever since I was a child, Grandma made it a point to read something to me until I learned how to read myself. Reading, as she described it, was power. She'd always tell me that knowledge was power, and reading was how a person obtained knowledge. Most Producers didn't read, and Grandma often told me that the more time went on, the more people would forget the English language... that they would speak in broken English. When people spoke funny or broke sentences up, she'd often lean into me and say, "See what happens when you don't read? You can't talk worth shit."

It always made me laugh. I liked the way Grandma spoke. It was so straightforward and funny. She described English from her time as laid back and creative. She said people would communicate about all sorts of things using unique words and that oftentimes, people would even make up words and they'd become official. Or at least, official *online*, whatever that meant.

It meant a lot when Grandma said that my vocabulary was good for a farmer. *Vast*, I think was the word she used.

Grandma grabbed me by the shoulders, kissed my forehead, and handed me a scrap piece of metal. "There, you're ready."

I grabbed the metal and stared at my distorted reflection. Although I wasn't used to seeing my hair tied back, I liked it. It stayed out of my face and made me look proper. I reached for it, touching my dark brown roots, and smiled. "This is great. Thank you, Grandma. And I smell wonderful."

She reached for my cheek and pinched it hard—something I always tried to avoid. "Yes, you do! And you look pretty damn good too, kiddo."

Kiddo.

I liked that.

No one else used this word, but Grandma always called me kiddo, so the word became special to me.

"What's goin' on here?" came Mother's voice.

I always hated when she barged into people's rooms. She did this often to me, and despite my room being only large enough for me to stick my arms out, it was still *my* bedroom.

With her hands on her hips, she gave me

the stink eye. "Silver, stop playin' around and get outside. The Elites are goin' to be here any minute."

Somedays, I hated how much I resembled my mother—green eyes, long dark brown hair, and skin neither pale nor dark. I had an athletic build like her, which she always criticized, and the same cheekbones, which weren't that prominent, but they were noticeable.

The only reason Mother even bothered to look interested in the Lottery was because she hoped that one day, if I won, I'd find a way to bring her into Olympus. She never seemed to think she'd win herself, and every time I asked her about it, she told me that it was disrespectful to question others and that I should mind my own business.

In fact, no one questioned Mother. There was a hardness to her that made everyone afraid of her.

Some days, I wondered if my father was taken to Olympus, which would explain why my mother was so bitter. But there was no way of knowing—she refused to talk to me about him, or about anything, really.

Even Grandma seemed on edge when I questioned her about it. She'd say that it was up to Mother to talk to me about it. I hated secrets more than the idea of living with the Elites.

Mother's tone hardened. "Get outside, now."

Grandma didn't seem too bothered by Mother's attitude, but I never liked annoying Mother, even if it felt like she hated me. Smiling at Grandma, I stood up and followed Mother outside toward the common area.

I wasn't one to visit the common area often—Mother rarely allowed it. It was where most Producers gathered to socialize after a long day of work. It was plain, with a dirt floor and many large stones to sit on. The space was large enough to fit several thousand bodies and sat right next to Division 9's main gates. Most people steered clear of the gate area, which was guarded by two heavily armed Defenders dressed in some scary red and black suits. Sometimes, little lights flashed on their suits. They must have been powered by something.

No one ever talked to the Defenders. They knew better. I'd heard of stories about their weapons being able to disintegrate people on the spot, and that was enough for me to keep my head down.

I preferred to disappear into my room and read after a long day in the garden beds.

Mother stormed through the crowd, elbowing everyone as she went. When people saw who she was, they didn't tell her to watch her step or to be careful. What were they so afraid of? Was Mother *that* cruel to everyone?

"At the front," she ordered, and I did as I was told.

The crowd continued to expand, filling the air around us with so much noise it was like being surrounded by huge swarms of flies. I stomped my way through the mud, my toes covered in a gooey brown—the result of heavy rainfall from the day before—until I found myself standing next to a boy my age with scraggly chestnut brown hair, light brown eyes, a flawless pale complexion, and hills for cheekbones that made it impossible for me to stop staring. He ran a hand through his hair, revealing a star-shaped scar on his wrist. It was odd. I'd never seen a mark like that before.

The moment he smiled at me, I bowed my head and looked away.

"First time?" he asked.

I didn't respond. I couldn't. I wasn't used to talking to people I didn't know.

At once, Mother nudged me in the back. "Silver, it's rude not to respond when spoken to. For God's sake, you'd think you would have learned that in those stupid books of yours."

This time, I made eye contact, and it looked like the boy felt sorry for me. He glanced at Mother, but only briefly. Not long enough to upset her.

"Y-yes," I said.

Again, he smiled. "You must have just had your seventeenth birthday."

Behind me, Mother sighed heavily as if the idea of my birthday was overwhelming. I'd never understood why she hated my birthday so much. I'd heard of children being celebrated on their birthdays. Grandma tried her best every year to make me feel special, but for some reason, Mother was always cruel with me on that day—more cruel than usual.

I nodded.

He could probably tell how uncomfortable I was. He reached out a hand. "I'm Rolie. Got transferred from Division 6 'bout a month ago."

Why was he giving me his hand? I stared at it, not knowing what to do.

"I–I'm Silver."

His lips pulled up on one side only. "Pleasure."

Behind me, Mother sighed.

Why did she always do that? It was embarrassing and made me so uncomfortable.

Rolie stared at my face. "I've seen you around here... I'd never forget a face like yours."

I sucked in a quick breath, my cheeks warming. I'd never seen *him* before. Were people too afraid to approach me because of Mother?

He parted his lips to say something, but all

of a sudden, Division 9's massive gates opened up, and through it came a lineup of Elites riding on white horses.

CHAPTER 3

I stared in awe as the Elites strode in with their backs straight and their chins pointed toward the sky. Their uniforms, white and stainless, looked like snow. It made me feel ugly with my torn hemp clothing and my filthy, scarred skin.

But my focus was on the horses. I'd never seen white ones like that before. I'd seen pictures of knights on white horses, but the images didn't do them justice.

It was incredible.

Grinning, I turned to Grandma, but my smile vanished when Mother jabbed me in the ribs, ordering me to focus.

The leader, a woman dressed in a similar white uniform with red stripes on her sleeves, led her horse to the front of the crowd. She smiled down at us and little lines formed next to her eyes—something Grandma referred to as crow's feet. She raised a hand to silence the crowd and watched us with such warmth that for a moment, I wondered what it might be like to live with the Elites.

She seemed nice enough. Maybe it wasn't all that bad.

If I won, would I have the same freedom Grandma has told me about all these years? Would I receive money to buy whatever I wanted? I chased these thoughts away. They were selfish. How could I possibly enjoy a life like that knowing that Grandma, along with countless other people, were being treated like slaves?

"Greetings, Division 9," the woman said.

Everyone bowed their heads and dropped to one knee. When I didn't budge, Mother dug her nails into the back of my neck. I winced and dropped down like everyone else. The air around me felt hot and thick. Everyone was quiet, holding their breaths.

Why?

Was this where they'd announce the lottery winner? I'd never attended Selection Day before—I'd never been allowed.

Rolie leaned into me. "That's Estrelle Marigold, chancellor for our division."

The woman was pretty but in an artificial way. Her skin looked like it was covered in something—a beige balm? I couldn't tell what it was, but it seemed that the intent was to mask her imperfections. Her hair, a golden blond, sat in a neat ball at the back of her head. It even shined under the sun as if coated with something.

She was thin, but seemed strong with square shoulders. Were those her real shoulders, or was that part of her uniform? I couldn't tell.

I stared at our chancellor, feeling small.

I'd read a few books on politics, including one about Lutum, to better understand how Olympus operated. Every division was assigned a chancellor who reported back to the president, meaning in total, ten chancellors oversaw all of Lutum.

I watched Estrelle as she spoke, her chest heaving and her fists wrapped firmly around the brown leather strap of her horse's bridle. She went on about how Division 9—also known as the division of agriculture—was formed, and how our obedience and hard work are what led to the rebirth of civilization. It felt recited, like she'd practiced this speech a hundred times before coming here.

Although I'd never attended Selection Day before, I remembered Grandma telling me about the beautiful horses, and how they were the only reason she would attend the celebration. She'd mentioned that despite Olympus having super-advanced technology, they made a point to attend Selection Day on horseback to remind the people of Lutum of the life they'd brought upon themselves—a simple life without technology.

Estrelle went quiet and wiggled in her seat, a little smirk pulling at the corner of her lips.

Was this it? Was she about to announce whether or not Division 9 had been selected? For the last few days, rumors had circulated in Lutum, but no one knew for sure if we'd won.

Everyone stood silently, and a swift breeze whistled through the crowd.

"I, Estrelle Marigold, would like to officially congratulate"—at once, the crowd exploded with cheering, but Estrelle continued, raising her voice as loud as she could—"on being selected to take part in the *Freedom Lottery!*"

My heart raced as the crowd became restless, and behind me, Mother dug her fingers into my shoulders, but not out of anger; it felt like she was holding her breath, hoping to the gods that I might be selected.

Estrelle grinned and pressed a hand over her heart. A man next to her guided his horse closer and handed her a slip of paper. It didn't look long. How come? Were there not many names on the list?

"Alicia Bloomsdale," she announced, and an isolated section of the crowd blew up with cries of joy.

"Annabelle Tyson."

"Singura Wilsif."

"Mark Yourk."

The names went on, and to my surprise, it was mostly young women that were selected except for a few young men not much older than me. I stared in horror, my clammy palms sticking to each other, when Rolie leaned in again and whispered, "You think they draw fairly? Sometimes I wonder if this thing is rigged."

Rigged? What did that even mean? I arched a brow at him.

"You know... fixed," he added.

I worried Mother might tell him to shut up, but she didn't. She stood quietly behind me, hanging on to Estrelle's every word.

"I don't understand what you're telling me," I whispered back.

"The Elites I've seen, aside from the Founders, are all really young," Rolie said.

By Founders, he meant the original members of Olympus—the first ones to receive the antiaging serum. Some of these members were well into their fifties and sixties by the time the drug was created, or at least that was what I'd heard. I'd never met a single Founder in person.

"I can't imagine them choosing anyone over the age of forty to join their society," he said.

When I didn't respond, he shook his head and waved dismissively. "Never mind."

As Estrelle continued to call out names, I swallowed hard. Why was I even nervous? It wasn't like I'd made any effort to earn points this past year. No way would I be included."

"Silverstasia Blackwood."

My head spun.

Had she... Had she called out my name? No way. I must have imagined it.

"Silver!" my mother shouted. She twirled me around so fast that my hair swept through the air and hit Rolie's face. Her eyes, round and wide, made me feel something I'd never felt from my mother before—love.

For the first time in my life, Mother looked happy. She looked proud.

"You did it! You're in the draw!" Saliva sprinkled from her mouth and onto the tip of my nose. She turned me around again, and before I could say anything, shoved me forward.

I stumbled, my arms swimming through the air, and joined the crowd of potential winners. As Estrelle continued to call out names, the crowd became even more frantic. It was like they knew the list was about to end, and some worried they might not be called.

"Luis Lamontagne," Estrelle shouted.

She crumpled the piece of paper and

slipped it into a tight pocket on her pant leg.

The crowd blew up in a rage, causing a few horses to neigh and jump back, their big hooves rising from the ground.

"Enough!" she shouted, and nodded at a Defender nearest to the crowd.

When no one listened, he extracted from his belt a gadget no larger than a pocketbook, and with his shoulders drawn back, aimed the weapon at the crowd.

No one dared make a sound after that.

Was this the same weapon I'd heard rumors about? The one that had disintegrated a Producer on the spot? I'd heard countless stories about how a man by the name of Peter Koris became so unruly that a Defender pressed a button, causing Peter to burst into a cloud of ash.

A story like that was frightening enough to make any person reconsider their behavior.

"My, my," Estrelle announced over the still crowd. "Is this how my people behave when they're awarded a gift? If so, I may simply have to reconsider placing your division into the draw next year, and perhaps even the year after that."

Several mouths parted, but no one spoke back.

Her forehead tightened, and she scanned the crowd with a sour expression. "Twenty hardworking individuals stand before you, deserving your praise and your respect."

As I watched Estrelle, I no longer saw the sweet, prideful woman from earlier. Instead, she reminded me of teachers I'd read about in some of my books—the ones who threatened and abused their students.

Her smile sprang back as quickly as it had vanished. "Now, shall we continue?"

The leather of her horse's saddle creaked as she climbed down, her matching leather boots landing softly in the mud. When it splashed up onto her pant leg, she curled her lips over her teeth as if someone had vomited on her.

She turned away from us and said, "Scramble, winners."

Everyone eyed each other, not quite understanding what this meant, until at last, a man with long braided hair and an unkempt beard pointed at us. "It's the same thing as last time," he said. "Mix yourselves up. Walk somewhere. Choose a different spot."

I did as instructed and navigated my way to the edge of my small group. Next to me, a young woman with a creamy brown face and bulging eyes trembled, her legs resembling twigs in the wind. I wanted to ask her if she was okay, but I was too scared to say anything.

When she caught me watching her, she forced a smile, then refocused her attention onto Estrelle. "Please pick me... please pick me... please pick me..." she mumbled, fidgeting with her fingers.

I searched the audience, where Mother stood with a scowl so hard you'd think some magical creature had turned her to stone. She didn't look angry, though. It was like she was concentrating and praying to every god she'd ever heard of to send good fortune my way.

Estrelle stood quietly with her back facing us. What was she doing? Why wasn't she moving?

A few moments passed and she raised an arm into the air. "One diamond, one beauty forever!"

Several gasps spread throughout the common area.

What was everyone so on edge about? Why was she holding her arm up like that?

In an instant, two clouds parted and a bright ray of sunlight came blasting down on all of us. It felt warm against my cheeks and neck, making me want to close my eyes and bathe in it. Instead, I watched Estrelle, wondering what her gestures signified, when I noticed something shiny between her thumb and index finger. It wasn't big or small—maybe the size of a grape, and it glowed the colors of a rainbow.

Was that the diamond she'd spoken of? I'd

read about diamonds in my books, but I'd never seen one in real life. It was magnificent.

"Eternal beauty, may you find the most deserving," she said, and she tossed the diamond toward us.

Squeals of excitement and fear filled our entire division as the diamond soared through the air, its fascinating rainbow colors making it impossible for me to look away. At first, it almost looked as though it might not reach us and instead land in the dirt, never to be found again.

But as it moved closer, I realized... it was coming straight toward me.

Was I dreaming? I couldn't possibly be the one selected to join the Elites in Olympus. I... I didn't want to be. My heart nearly stopped when the stone landed in the dirt next to my bare feet, and the entire audience sucked in what sounded like a single, giant breath.

Estrelle spun on her feet and raised a flat palm that I was certain signified, *Nobody move.*

So I stood still, staring wide-eyed at the diamond in the mud.

The closer she came, the faster my heart raced. She looked even taller off her horse, with long slender legs and an elongated torso. Unsmiling, she pursed her lips the way Mother did when she was concentrating and came close to me.

When she reached us, a spicy floral scent filled my nostrils and my knees almost buckled. I'd never smelled anything like that before. Was that what perfume smelled like? I breathed in hard again, wanting to hold onto this smell forever.

Estrelle's piercing blue eyes landed on me, the diamond, and then the girl next to me.

My stomach sank.

Was I... Was I the winner? Or was the other girl the winner?

"Did I win?" asked the dark-skinned girl who'd been trembling earlier.

Then, someone else in the crowd said, "It's between them both! Who won?"

Estrelle's jaw muscles popped out on either side. She seemed upset, but I didn't understand why.

"No, it's in front of this girl," she said, pointing at me.

"I don't think so—" someone else said.

"It's a tie!" someone cried out.

"No, it isn't—" Estrelle tried.

"It's a tie!" someone else shouted.

Without smiling, Estrelle stiffened her posture and clicked her fingers at someone behind her. I wasn't sure who she was calling until the man on the horse next to her climbed down. He moved toward us with one hand behind his back.

"Yes?" he asked.

Turning away from us, she leaned into his ear and whispered something.

The man tilted his head sideways to look at the diamond.

"What's going on?" came a whisper from the audience.

"Who won?"

"It can't be a tie!"

"Silence!" Estrelle shouted. Veins bulged from her temples and several strands spilled forward from her perfectly coiffed hair.

Anger didn't suit her, and when she realized we were staring at her, she ran a hand over her hair to flatten the loose strands back into whatever product held everything in place. Then she smiled so big that her molars appeared.

"Agrul, please provide me with the measurements," she said. "Surely, this isn't a tie. It appears to be more on the right."

The Elite standing next to her, Agrul, reached into his pocket and extracted a long band with writing on it. A measuring tape? It was much nicer than the ones we made here in Division 9.

Crouching, he placed the measuring tape next to the diamond and measured several places: the space between the diamond and my foot and the space between the diamond and the other girl. He did this another three times because Estrelle kept telling him to remeasure when he'd look back at her. Every time he measured, his gloved hand tickled my bare foot.

Eventually, he sighed, got up, and shook his head.

Estrelle looked like she was about to blow up. But with everyone watching her, she forced yet another smile, repositioned her white overcoat, cleared her throat, and said, "For the first time in history... it would appear we have a tie."

"I knew it!" someone shouted.

Before the crowd could blow up again, she stuck out a flat palm. She seemed confident in what she was doing, but she did that thing with her lips again, and I knew she was working hard to figure it all out in her head.

The dark-skinned girl next to me trembled so severely her teeth clattered. "I-I-I" she stammered, unable to get a full word out.

Without thinking, I opened my mouth. "She can have it."

Estrelle's eyes bulged. "I beg your pardon?"

I swallowed hard and avoided eye contact with Mother. "I-I'll give my win to her. She can have it."

Estrelle's mouth clamped shut, her teeth smacking together.

Agrul stared at her, looking just as confused. Had I made a mistake? Should I have waited to see if I might be selected to be an Elite? It didn't matter. The truth was, I didn't want to be an Elite. I didn't want to leave Grandma behind.

Estrelle's overcoat folded as she leaned toward me. Instinctively, I leaned back, not wanting her face so close to mine.

"That is a bold thing to say..." she breathed, her minty breath entering my nostrils. "What is your name?" She reached for my face, but I pulled away.

"Silver," I said.

She narrowed her eyes on me, deep lines spreading across her face. "And why on Earth would you refuse immortality, Silver?"

My eyes darted toward the crowd, and that's when I saw her. Mother. Only, she didn't look like Mother. She looked like a monster... like a demon from hell. Her dark hair, wiry and muddy, made her look deathly pale. Her eyes, usually jade green like mine and Grandma's, looked black under her protruding brows. She curled her lip over her front teeth and scowled at me like she was trying to murder me with her mind.

Maybe this had been a mistake, after all. Mother would never forgive me for this. But when I caught Grandma's soft eyes, I felt confident in my decision.

"I want to stay here," I said. "With my family."

Estrelle smirked, but it felt fake. It was the kind of smile someone gets when they're enraged and doing everything in their power to hold back an outburst.

She must have thought I was delusional for giving up a life in Olympus. Maybe she didn't understand anything about family.

Sighing, she pushed on her knees and stood straight. "Suit yourself, Silver."

She turned to the girl next to me, who I thought might die of a heart attack, and said, "What might your name be?"

"A-A-Annabelle T-T-T-yson."

Estrelle quickly composed herself, though it was apparent by the way she cringed that she hated stuttering. Either that, or she hated any form of extreme emotion.

"Come," she ordered, and Annabelle followed her toward the horses, her legs wobbly.

When they'd reached the front of the crowd, Estrelle grabbed Annabelle's tiny wrist and raised it so high that Annabelle stood on her tippy toes.

"Annabelle Tyson, Elite of Olympus!" she shouted, and the crowd went wild.

As clapping and cheering erupted

throughout Division 9, Estrelle led Annabelle toward a carriage near the gates. I stood still as countless eyes turned on me. What were they thinking? That I'd lost my mind? I didn't care. I felt like I'd made the right decision, and I was prepared to defend it.

The crowd became so loud and distracting that I didn't notice her at first. It was only when she drew in nearer that I saw her—Mother. She ran toward me with her fingers curled and her mouth agape, shouting things I couldn't hear. Her face, ghost white only moments ago, was now so red that it might as well have been dripping with beet juice.

As she ran toward me, I couldn't move. I wanted to run, but I couldn't.

"Fool... ish... g... l!"

Her words became more audible the closer she got, and her mouth seemed to open wider and wider with every venomous word.

"You foolish girl! What have you done? You're dead! Do you hear me?"

Right before she lunged at me, several men managed to grab her and pin her to the ground. She shook violently under them, mud splashing all over her face, and shouted things that didn't make any sense. Had I broken her? Had she snapped?

Estrelle, seemingly disgusted by Mother's behavior, walked toward us, rubbing her thumb and index finger together as if the sight of my mother were enough to make her feel dirty.

"What is the meaning of this?" she asked Mother.

"She's an abomination!" Mother shouted, her voice a throaty growl.

Still calm, Estrelle pressed the heel of her leather boot on top of Mother's hand. Something crunched, and Mother shouted out in pain.

"You will do well to mind your behavior," Estrelle said, eyes aimed at Mother's monstrous face. "Should I receive word that you laid a hand on this girl, you will lose your head."

Mother breathed out hard, her teeth clenched.

Why was Estrelle defending me? She didn't even know me. I wanted to thank her, but I knew it was best to keep my mouth shut.

"Do you understand?" Estrelle said, adding more weight against Mother's hand.

"Yes!" Mother cried out.

Smiling, Estrelle pulled away, returned to her horse, and mounted it. "Keep up the wonderful work, everyone. You have made the Elites very happy this year."

Everyone beamed as if blessed by the gods.

It made me sick to my stomach.

Guiding her horse toward the gates, Estrelle waved a hand above her head. "I shall see you all again soon."

CHAPTER 4

Supper was unusually quiet that night in our home.

Grunwalt didn't speak a word about the selection that day, and for the first time in as long as I'd known him, he didn't go on about how *everything would be fine*, or how *it was time to start preparing for next year's lottery.*

Kiatha kept quiet next to the open hearth, her dark face glistening behind the dancing flames. I ate my cold soup in silence, wondering if Mother would ever return to normal. She'd disappeared into her bedroom and closed the holey curtain for privacy. Despite Grandma telling her to seek medical attention, Mother refused. She said her broken fingers would heal on their own. It wasn't like she had much of a choice. Medical care was limited in Lutum, and only those in serious condition received treatment. Even then, most didn't make it.

I joined Kiatha by the fire and stuck out my bowl of soup, allowing the flames to warm my hands.

"Quite the day you had, child," she said.

I nodded and sat on the wooden log beside her. It shifted as my weight came down, but I was used to it. I sipped the cold beef broth off the tip of my wooden spoon, appreciating the salty taste against my tongue. The fire's flames warmed my skin, though it made my soup taste colder. My eyes became dry and hot as I stared into the flames. I could sense Kiatha observing me, but I didn't look up at her.

After a beat, she said, "You don't owe anyone an explanation, ya hear me?"

I tried to nod, but my head barely moved. While I appreciated her words, I wasn't quite sure they were true. I got the feeling that everyone would soon be demanding an explanation from me. Why wouldn't they? No one had ever refused immortality before.

I would be bombarded with questions daily.

Why would you do something like that?

Aren't you miserable here, Silver?

What a shame you've brought onto your family.

I'd probably earn a few nicknames, too, such as The Girl Who Chose to Age, or, The Girl Who Rejected Eternal Life, or, The Girl Who Refused Immortality.

Maybe people would start calling me worse things. Maybe they'd call me insane or say that I'd lost my wits.

How long would the attention last? I wanted to be left alone.

I thanked Kiatha for her kindness and left to my room, then closed the stained curtain behind me. I lay in my bed—an uncomfortable block constructed of hay and cotton sheets—and stared at the clay ceiling, imagining what it might be like to be a character in one of my fiction books. Most days, evenings were what I looked forward to the most. They were the only time I could escape reality and see the world through someone else's eyes. I craned my neck and peeked toward my curtain to ensure no one was looking, then reached for the paperback book stuffed inside my pillow: 1984 by George Orwell.

If Mother found the book, she'd either rip it apart or burn it. She'd done it before, which infuriated me so much. The few books we had in Lutum had been passed down from generation to generation and kept secret from the Defenders. Aside from memories shared by our elders, books were our only source of knowledge and education. I couldn't understand why Mother would want to take that away from me.

With the book in my hands, I stared out

through the open window of my room—a tiny square the size of a plate—and watched quietly as a fly landed on the clay sill. It buzzed, its tiny translucent wings flicking every few seconds.

Was I the only one who thought the Elites were corrupt? I felt so alone. Maybe something was wrong with me. Everyone else in Lutum seemed to think the Elites should be revered.

A gentle tap shook me from my trance and I shoved the book under my pillow.

"C-come in," I said, my heart racing.

Grandma's sweet, wrinkled face and salt-and-pepper hair slipped past the curtain. With a limp, she approached my tiny bed and sat at the edge.

I wanted to hug her... to cry, to scream. Anything. But emotions weren't tolerated in Lutum. I needed to compose myself.

"Are you all right, kiddo?" she whispered.

The words came out as if they were illegal, almost as if discussing one's feelings were punishable by death. Why? Weren't feelings part of being human? Why was it so shameful to express them?

I shrugged with one shoulder, and Grandma laid a hand on my lap. She was the only one to ever show me affection, even if only in private. It meant the world to me. A single touch from her made me feel safe, warm, and whole.

"I don't understand," I said. "I didn't even produce well this year. How did I end up in the selection?"

Her lips sagged downward, and I got the feeling she felt awful about what had happened. Responsible, even.

"I'm sorry, sweetheart. All I've ever wanted for you was a better life... A life away from all of this. You deserve that, Silver."

I met her wet gray-green eyes, trying to understand what she meant. She spoke as if she had influence over what had happened today.

When she didn't look away, it hit me.

"Grandma, did you—"

Her loving smile returned. "My points are no good to me, kiddo. Look at me." She pinched the loose skin under her chin and wiggled it, making me smile. "I'm old. And from what we've been told, the serum doesn't reverse aging, it only stops it. Besides, I've lived my life. You're young. You deserve to be happy."

"I'm happy here with you," I said.

She reached for my face—a warm caress that made me want to rest my head inside her palm and go to sleep.

"This world is never going to change unless people are willing to change it," she said.

I didn't understand. What could someone like me possibly do to change the world? To change Olympus... and Lutum?

"How did you give me your points?" I asked.

It wasn't like they were transferrable. This didn't make any sense.

"I gave you the credit when completing the production forms," she said. "A few extra crops here and there helped boost your score."

I couldn't believe that Grandma would do something like that. The Elites took production seriously and hated dishonesty. Grandma had risked her life by sharing some of her points with me, which only made me feel worse. She'd tried so hard to get me into Olympus, and I'd walked away from my only chance. For the first time that day, I regretted my decision. "You did this for me... I shouldn't have backed out of the draw."

Her eyes narrowed into drooping moons. "Don't you worry, Silver. What you did today is going to change everything."

"I don't understand."

She leaned in and kissed my forehead. "You will. Now, get some sleep, kiddo. Tomorrow's gonna be a crazy day for you."

Smirking, I rolled my eyes. "I bet."

She stood up, grabbing her lower back. Poor Grandma. She was always in so much pain. Here in Lutum, it didn't matter if you were old or even disabled. Everyone worked. And when you couldn't work anymore, you were targeted by the Defenders. On more than one occasion, I'd witnessed Defenders beat the elderly, telling them to get their asses back to work.

It disgusted me.

How was everyone so excited for a lottery that occurred once every year, while the rest of the year was spent living in horrible conditions?

Hope.

That was what everyone held onto. Blind hope.

Before Grandma exited my bedroom, she turned to me and winked. "Fiction is often inspired by the real world, Silver. Make sure you finish that book before your mother finds it."

Smiling, I reached for my book again, and Grandma closed the curtain.

CHAPTER 5

I stared at the poster, trying to understand what had people so excited. The paper, a yellow-brown sheet with curled edges, showed a picture of two Elites—one male, one female—standing proudly with balled fists on their hips.

It was a stance that reminded me of the superheroes I learned about in the few comics I'd ever read. It wasn't long before those were thrown in the village fire. Atop the two lottery winners was a bold header that read *This Could Be You.*

"This could be you," I muttered, mockingly. Under the picture was text:

- You will never age
- You will live among the most educated, prestigious, and wealthy people on Earth
- You will live as a god
- You will never want for anything

I supposed it did sound appealing. Imagine never wanting for anything? Still, reading the poster made me sick to my stomach. There was something very wrong with our system.

"This could be you..." I mocked again.

"Could it?" came a familiar voice.

I spun around to find Rolie standing next to me with arms crossed over his fruit-stained shirt. He smiled crookedly and tilted his head.

"Are you following me?" I asked.

"Me?" he said. "Following *you*? If I wanted to follow a crazy person, I'd pick someone less—" he eyed me from top to bottom— "strange."

I clenched a fist, prepared to punch him in the shoulder when two Defenders walked past us. I quickly composed myself. Did he think he was funny? I didn't find him funny.

"I'm only teasing you," he said. "Why are you reading the lottery poster?"

I breathed out through my nostrils. "Trying to make sense of my decision."

"Well," he said, "I think you made the right decision."

I scoffed. "Is that why everyone's staring at me?"

Around us, countless eyes darted between us, the Defenders, and the garden beds. It was like they were waiting for something to happen... something dramatic.

His smile disappeared. "Attention ain't always a bad thing, Silver. You can use it for good."

His eyes darted toward the Defenders and his jaw muscles popped.

Did he feel the same way about the Elites as I did? If so, he'd never admit it. No one could admit it.

"Do y'know what those things are?" he asked, shooting a glance at the lamppost across the dirt path.

"I may not have gone to school like our ancestors," I said, a bit insulted, "but I know what a lamppost is."

He ran a hand through his hair and held back a smirk. "I know you aren't an idiot, Silver. You're the opposite, if ya ask me. Smarter than all o' us. You speak better than—"

"What's your point about the light?" I asked.

"See, took me a while to figure it out," he said, "but you see those?"

The second I turned to look, his fingers caught my cheek. "Don't look now. You'll make it obvious. I think they use those to watch us."

"Like cameras?" I asked.

He slapped a hand over my mouth, and at once, a deep, authoritative voice shouted, "Hands off!"

Rolie pulled away and raised his hands. "We're only playing around."

"Back to work!" the Defender shouted.

Rolie laughed through his nose. "Funny how they'll let ya have a break if you're starin' at the poster, hopin' for a better life... but the second ya start havin' a real conversation with someone, alls they do is get in your face about it."

"Now!" the voice commanded.

Footsteps stomped across the dirt and Rolie rushed back to his post.

Although tempted, I didn't glance up at the light. I'd do it later. I quickly glanced at the Defender, who stared at me from behind a black shield of glass over his face. As I ran to our post, where Grandma, Mother, Kiatha, and Grunwalt were rummaging through bushes on their hands and knees, I sensed everyone's eyes on me.

It was like the Producers of Division 9 were waiting for me to do something... anything.

What did they think would happen? I'd made one decision, and now they looked at me as if I held the key to something important.

When I joined Grandma's side, I plucked cherry tomatoes and green beans and filled up her wicker basket. Every time we filled one up, the Defenders came by, scooped them up, and placed them on a horse-drawn cart. It was upsetting to see all of our crops taken out through the gates for Olympus. We were left with spotted potatoes, soft leeks, and occasionally, overripe fruit.

Supper that night went the same as it had the night before. It was cold, and Mother was absent. When I finished eating, I placed my bowl on our kitchen's wooden table. As I turned away, prepared to wish everyone a good night, a gentle knock came from the front door.

Everyone froze, their spoons floating midair, and Grandma placed her hands on her knees, prepared to get up.

No one ever knocked around this time of day. The sun was setting, which meant any minute now, the Defenders would begin enforcing curfew.

"I'll get it," I said.

I hurried to the door and with one eye pressed against the crack, creaked it open.

Rolie stood on the other side, his torn boots full of mud.

I frowned at him. "What are you doing here?"

He offered that same smug look he'd given me earlier, only this time, he raised what appeared to be a giant mushroom, only it didn't exactly look like a deformed mushroom.

"What is that?" I asked. I'd never seen anything like it.

On top of it was some sort of jelly. Strawberry, maybe, and at the center of this jelly was a beige wax candle with its wick lit on fire.

"Happy belated birthday," he said. "They call this a cupcake."

The cold leek soup in my stomach instantly felt warm. No one had ever done anything like this for me before. I couldn't help but smile as I watched the bright orange flame dance from side to side.

"A cupcake," I repeated dreamily. I wasn't used to smiling, and it made the muscles of my face feel tired. "Wow, um, thank you—"

I opened the door wider, prepared to reach for this strange *cupcake* when a firm hand grabbed the back of my neck.

"What's the meanin' o' this?" came Mother's voice.

She stormed out of the house, grabbed the cupcake, and threw it next to Rolie's feet. It splattered, its decorative berries spreading across my bare feet like blood.

"Mother!" I shouted.

"Who do you think you are?" she snapped at Rolie. With her good hand, she shoved his chest, and he stumbled backward.

"I-I'm sorry, ma'am," he said. "I meant no disrespect."

She slapped the air in front of him. "Get outta here, ya good for nothin' scoundrel!"

I clenched my teeth, rage building inside

me. How could she be so cruel? Not only had she never celebrated my birthday, but she cursed anyone who tried to.

Rolie didn't deserve that. My face heated with embarrassment.

I should have kept my mouth shut and disappeared into my room, but I couldn't. With so much anger inside me, I feared if I didn't let it out, I might lose my head.

"You're a monster!" I shouted.

Her features hardened, and with her good hand, she slapped me across the face. It tingled, burned, and even hurt, but it didn't compare to the darkness I felt on the inside.

With clenched teeth, she said, "You should be grateful you're even alive, you filthy abomination!"

I wanted to slap her back or yell at her for being so awful. But I couldn't. Instead, my throat swelled, and before tears could come sliding down my face, I ran to my room. Behind me, Mother and Grandma bickered, but I started crying too loudly to hear what they were arguing about.

I cried myself to sleep that night, holding onto the image of Rolie and his cupcake.

CHAPTER 6

"Silver, wake up," came Grandma's voice. She shook me from side to side. "Silver!" I cracked my eyes open. Grandma stared at me with big folds across her forehead.

"What's going on?" I asked.

"The Elites are back," she said. "Everyone knows the Elites only visit us twice a year—once for the lottery, and once for a midyear check-in. Something's up."

Why on Earth would they return a few days after the lottery? Had something happened? I shot out of bed and slipped into my day clothes. I hadn't washed them in over two weeks, but they weren't too stained. I could get away with a few more days.

"Come," Grandma said.

Together, we ran out to the common area, our feet breaking through the morning fog. The sun, only now rising above the horizon, made my tired eyes squint.

People all around us bickered back and forth. They were probably wondering the same thing as me. What was going on? There weren't as many Elites this time. It didn't feel as... ceremonial. Estrelle led Agrul and one other rider toward us, and behind them was the same horse-drawn carriage that had taken Annabelle away.

As Estrelle rode forward, she raised a flat palm, silencing everyone. "Silverstasia Blackwood, step forward."

I swallowed hard. Was this it? Was I going to be punished for having defied the Elites? For having made fools of them?

I didn't want to approach the front, but I didn't have a choice. Everyone around me stepped away as if I were infected with leprosy. Bowing my head, I took a step forward.

"Silverstasia Blackwood," Estrelle announced. "President Kane has personally requested you join the Elites." Smiling sweetly, she extended a gloved hand, inviting me to approach.

Was this some sort of trap? Why was the president involved? It wasn't like I'd changed my mind.

"Um, no thank you," I said, and gasps sucked the air from all around me.

She curled her upper lip as if having licked a lemon. "No... thank you?" she repeated in disgust. "Young girl, we do not tolerate black sheep among Lutum! You are hereby ordered to approach at once."

"But I—" I tried, and without warning, four Defenders ran toward me and grabbed me by the arms. "No, please!"

I tried to kick and pull away, but it was no use. They were too strong. I was powerless. As I approached Estrelle's side, she looked at me as if I were filth. "You, my child, have made a grave mistake."

"But I—Grandma!" I shouted.

It was no use.

No one was coming to defend me. They were too scared. Instead, everyone watched me, terrified. Why wasn't anyone helping? They were taking me against my will. This wasn't what I wanted.

The carriage door was opened and I was thrown inside. I landed on my hands and knees, my arms tender from having been squeezed so hard by the Defenders.

Behind me, a latch locked, and I was left alone in the darkness.

What was happening? I thought joining the Elites was meant to be a pleasant experience. Why were they treating me like a prisoner? Because I had rejected their offer?

Was that their plan? To imprison me for making them look like fools? Slowly, I crawled my way up onto the seating area—a wooden bench covered with a red, soft cushion that looked like it had been sewn for a king or a queen. In the middle of the carriage door, next to the bench, was a small window with metal bars. I inched closer to it, wrapped my fingers around the bars, and pressed my face against the cold metal.

The crowd stared quietly, likely as confused as I was.

Estrelle turned her horse around, prepared to lead the carriage back to Olympus when a man stepped out from the crowd and shouted, "What are you going to do with her? She's only a girl!"

Midturn, Estrelle clenched her jaw. She pulled on her horse's leather reins and turned back to face the crowd.

"Why, Silver is going to become an Elite," she said.

That same man—an older gentleman with scabs and scars all over his body—jabbed a stiff finger in my direction. "I thoughts the lottery were supposed ta be a gift... a prize. Seems ta me like you're takin' this girl 'gainst her will."

For a moment, Estrelle didn't say anything. She sat with her back stiff and her knuckles white around her reins. Although I couldn't see her face, I imagined her left eyelid fluttering. Finally, she said, "This is a special circumstance, and I can assure you—"

"Assure us?" came Mother's voice.

Mother.

Why was she getting involved? What did she care?

"How can we be sure my daughter will even be given the serum? You're taking her like she's a prisoner. This isn't right. It isn't right! You let her go at once!"

The crowd around her automatically blew up. Men and women shouted all sorts of things and pointed fingers at the Elites.

"Liars!"

"Scoundrels!"

At once, four Defenders stepped forward with their black-gloved hands hovering beside their weapons belts.

"No," Estrelle said. "Leave them be." She raised her chin and cleared her throat. "You may all consider yourselves removed from next year's lottery!"

When Estrelle turned back around, I saw something I'd never seen before—fear. It was like she knew she'd made a mistake. Either that, or she hadn't expected such a violent reaction. The crowd became wild, throwing mud into the air like a bunch of baboons. Two men even charged forward as if preparing to rescue me from my prison, but the moment they were near, one of the Defenders whipped out a gadget and pointed it at them.

The two men stopped dead in their tracks, their arms pinned across each other's chests like they were trying to protect each other from Defender. But it was pointless. As they stepped back, surrendering, the Defender pressed a button.

Screams filled the common area as both men were burned alive within seconds. It happened so fast that it was impossible to tell if they'd suffered. They collapsed, ashes falling from their skeletal frames.

Behind them, women cried and pleaded, one of them running out toward the piles of ashes.

"No, no! What have you done?" she shouted, her eyes moist and bloodshot.

Estrelle gave the Defender a nasty glare—one that said, *You disobeyed a direct order.*

She knew there was no coming back from this. With her head held high, she kicked her horse's sides and rushed to the front of the carriage.

"To Olympus, now."

CHAPTER 7

The ride to Olympus felt like an eternity. My butt and back ached—so much so that I had to shift the weight of my body every few seconds. How far away was this place?

We rode for hours until something shimmered through the carriage window.

Rubbing my eyes, I moved closer and peered outside.

It was... what was the word? *Magnificent.*

All around us was plush grass, its blades thick and emerald green. Never in my life had I seen grass this *wow* before. The only grass we had in Lutum consisted of random patches around the garden, and most of it grew knee high before a Producer cut it with sheers. I'd heard of grass growing in Division 5, where livestock were raised, but those were only rumors.

Across these massive fields of green were

cedar hedges—something I'd only ever read about. They were trimmed perfectly, some with oval shapes and others, perfect squares. They stood in precise alignment on either side of a clear path that appeared made of stone. Or was that... cobblestone?

It was as if someone had knelt and taken hours to place perfectly shaped stones side by side until they formed a path. I couldn't believe how nice it looked. I wondered how it felt under the pads of one's foot. Was it as soft as dirt? As wood? Did it get slippery in the rain?

The second we got onto the path, the carriage began to rattle. It tickled the pads of my bare feet, making me lift them onto the seat. It was the strangest feeling, and I wasn't sure whether I liked it or hated it.

I hoped there would still be cobblestones when we arrived in Olympus. I wanted to know what they felt like against my feet. Would I even be allowed to walk around, or would I be confined in a small space and left to starve?

These thoughts disappeared when Olympus came into view. It was so fascinating that my jaw went slack. It was... *mesmerid*. Or *mesmerizing*. I couldn't remember the word. But the beauty that lay up ahead made me want to never look away.

At the far end of the cobblestone path was a gigantic city. It sparkled under the sun's bright glow. Massive gray stone walls protected the city, which was so vast I couldn't even see the city's sides.

How many people lived in Olympus?

I blinked hard and smiled big as two huge crystalline gates were opened, seemingly by magic. Was this what *technology* was capable of? Opening doors? I'd never seen anything like it in my life.

Grasping the iron bars of my prison, I stared out in wonder as we entered the gates.

We rode into the city, and in my excitement, I pressed my face even harder into the bars. We passed tons of large structures built of all sorts of materials. I couldn't tell what they were. Some sort of stone. Walls were so polished they looked wet. Some of the buildings stood so tall that I couldn't wrap my head around how they had been constructed.

No matter how much I pushed my face into the metal bars, I couldn't see the roofs of some buildings.

And the streets... they were nothing like ours. Rather than dirt and mud, they were constructed of white polished stones, laid side by side. They blended so perfectly that they looked like one giant piece. Everywhere I turned, colorful flowers brought a smile to my face.

People walked in the streets, smiling and

laughing. Unlike in Lutum, their clothes were all unique. No one wore the same thing. Some men were dressed in bright blue button-up suits, while others wore green and purple and even yellow. Some women wore dresses, others, pantsuits, their colors as varied as the flowers around them.

I reached for my shirt, and my finger slid through a small tear. Would they give me clothing of my own to replace these?

One woman laughed—a sound I wasn't used to hearing—and fixed the pineapple-like shape atop her head. I couldn't tell if she was wearing a hat, or if this was her hair. And if it was her hair, how did she manage to keep it up so neatly? And how was everyone's hair so... clean? Skin tones varied as much as flowers— brown, yellow, beige, black, all of which were clean and dirt-free.

As we swept through the city, people moved aside, kneeling and bowing as we passed.

Who were they bowing at? Estrelle? Was she considered royalty among the Elites? I'd always imagined everyone being royalty here. Maybe there were different classes.

The smell of crisp, hot meat flooded my nostrils. It smelled salty and sweet at the same time. I stuck my nose out through the bars, inhaling as much of it as I could. That was when

I saw it—a long road filled with what appeared to be... stores. At least, I thought they were, based on how Grandma had described them to me.

People gathered all around them, some coming out with items in their arms, others with bags full of clothing. Some people even ate food as they walked down the path.

What were they eating? What I wouldn't have done for a bite of—

"Hot dogs, get your hot dogs!" one man shouted.

Hot... dog? My eyes nearly popped out of my skull. I'd always heard about dogs being loyal companions. Why would anyone want to eat one?

I watched as a woman approached the man selling hot dogs. Around her wrist was a thin bracelet, and she placed this over a gadget owned by the hot dog seller. What was she doing? When she pulled away, the man gave her what looked like a tube of meat within two slices of bread. Or, maybe it was one piece of bread folded in two.

I couldn't tell.

My stomach grumbled as I caught one last glimpse of the woman biting into the hot, juicy meat sandwich.

We rode past more buildings, most of which I knew nothing about, and outdoor areas filled with adults and children. The children ran around with rosy cheeks, throwing balls around and playing with them.

Everyone seemed so... happy.

The texture of the ground suddenly changed—I felt it in the rumbling of the carriage. When I looked outside, my stomach sank.

Below us was a body of water with thousands of ripples dancing across its surface.

We were crossing a bridge. But to where?

At long last, we came to a stop, and I rushed over to the other window to peer through. Ahead of us was a building so large and beautiful that I had to blink several times to make sure I wasn't imagining it.

Was that a castle?

Dozens of towers that looked like glass stood tall, the sun's reflection making the structure look like a giant, sparkling diamond. Platforms moved up and down behind the glass, floating as if by magic. Atop the platforms were people, and from here, they looked like ants.

Were those elevators? I'd read about them but never imagined them to look like that.

From behind the glass, thousands of blue lights flickered. I couldn't figure out what they were, but they resembled stars across a moonlit sky.

I nearly choked on my saliva when a small, silver gadget came buzzing next to my window. It floated in midair, a humming sound escaping small dots beneath its belly. At the center was an illuminated blue circle, similar to an eye.

It beeped again before disappearing toward Estrelle.

"Yes, we have her," Estrelle said to the flying gadget.

I couldn't believe my eyes.

Was I dreaming?

The carriage shook once more as we moved forward and entered the castle.

CHAPTER 8

I stared in wonder as the carriage rode through what appeared to be a courtyard. The ground, an even slab of stone, looked like it might be cool against the pads of my feet. Around us, walls as tall as the sky boxed us in, but there was no ceiling. I craned my neck, sticking my nose out of the window, and gazed up at the puffy clouds as they floated by.

At the center of the courtyard was a fountain that looked like a statue of Poseidon, or at least what I imagined Poseidon looking like based on the descriptions I'd read. Water flowed from his trident and trickled down around the base of his feet. There, birds bathed, shaking their heads and wings from side to side.

I smiled.

I couldn't remember the last time I'd seen a bird.

The carriage stopped abruptly and I waited,

my heart pounding. Would they finally retrieve me from my prison? Estrelle's voice carried in the distance. I couldn't tell what she was saying, but it had sounded like an announcement, or maybe an order.

At once, the carriage took off again, this time making a left turn. We disappeared through a tall archway made of stone, and the natural sunlight disappeared as we entered an enclosed space. A tunnel? Why was it so dark? Where were they taking me? I'd have much preferred to stay out in the courtyard.

The rattling started again, which meant we'd climbed back onto the cobblestones.

The air became cool and humid, and I grew uncomfortable.

Was I being taken into a room underground?

Dim lights hung from the ceiling, illuminating the dark space. We descended downward, the carriage gaining speed as we followed a twirling path. The speed became so great that I slid over to the left of the seat, my shoulder smashing into the carriage's sidewall.

When we stopped, the air felt even colder. It smelled of dirt, combined with something clean, and citrus-like—lemon, maybe.

"As requested," Estrelle announced. "Yes, the daughter. That's right."

The daughter? Were they talking about me?

And if so, what did me being my mother's daughter have anything to do with this? I hoped they hadn't harmed her after I left.

The carriage latch unexpectedly shifted and the door opened wide. Was this an invitation to step out? I wasn't certain, so I didn't move until a man dressed in a bright white uniform, slick black hair, and a clean-shaven face stepped forward. He held a metallic slab in his perfectly groomed hands. The slab shimmered, reflecting light, and with his index finger, he tapped the shiny surface. More lights flashed as he did this and text and images appeared. It was as if he were controlling the images with his touch.

What was that thing?

His eyes, black as coal behind a pair of brown-rimmed glasses, remained fixated on the gadget in front of him. The piece of technology cast a blue hue up across his chin, cheeks, and forehead and even reflected off his glasses.

He didn't look old—maybe around my age— but acted quite oddly. He was stiff and proper, almost in an inhuman way. He tilted his head to the side and smiled at me—a crooked smile that expanded a small pink scar over his lips. "I'm Adam. I'll be your escort."

"Adam," I repeated. "I'm—"

"Silver," he said with a smooth voice.

"You're new here. Follow me."

His English was good. Did people here go to school?

Reluctantly, I held onto the wall of the carriage, crouched, and stepped out through the open door. My feet landed softly on red cobblestones, but I refused to let go of the carriage behind me. Without giving me much attention, he twirled on his shiny shoes and walked toward a door that seemed made of black metal. It was shiny and hard-looking— nothing like our doors in Lutum.

With a flick of his wrist, the door swept open.

How... How had he done that?

He'd told me to follow, but I couldn't move. Why couldn't I follow him? Any minute now, a group of Defenders would take me by force, accusing me of being a disobedient little brat.

Go on, Silver, follow him.

Estrelle and Agrul sat on their horses at the front, discussing something. Not once did they bother to look my way. What if I ran? I glanced behind me, down the narrow tunnel that curved until all I saw was blackness.

I could try.

It would take them some effort to turn their horses around in a narrow place like this, and maybe I'd even find a secret door along the way.

But as I thought of running for my life, the carriage behind me shifted, and its wheels began to turn.

Wait. Where were they going? The carriage wheels shook and rattled as Estrelle disappeared into the darkness up ahead.

I was alone, standing in front of an open door. The man, Adam, was nowhere to be seen. Deep down, I knew running was foolish. If the Elites had the technology to open doors on their own, surely, it wouldn't be hard for them to track me down.

So I entered the open doorway, terrified.

"We do not tolerate disobedience here, Miss Blackwood."

I jumped at the sound of his voice and turned to my right. There he stood, illuminated by a strange-looking light above his head. It didn't look like fire, and it didn't give off a yellow hue the way our streetlights did in Lutum. It was much colder looking. Was this artificial light? Electricity? I stared in awe, my jaw dropping.

Adam reached for something on the wall, and one by one, more lights turned on, filling the air with a soft humming sound. Why were the lights making noise?

"Welcome to Olympus," he said with a childlike grin. "Take a seat near intake and someone will be with you soon."

When I didn't respond, he hesitated, his eyes darting from side to side. "Um, Miss Blackwood"—he extended a palm toward the seating area—"right there."

I scanned the room, a huge space with high ceilings and multicolored lights flickering everywhere. I blinked hard, my eyes trying to acclimate themselves to the artificial atmosphere. Metal-framed chairs formed rows throughout the open space, almost as if waiting for an audience, or an entire village, to sit. They weren't quite aimed at anything... mostly at each other. I'd seen images of rooms like this before, and I immediately thought of a subway or train station.

At the center of the room was a structure in the shape of a hectogon. Glass windows sat evenly around the frame, and at the front was an open window. Right below this was a wooden shelf about the height of my chest.

As I moved closer to the sitting area, Adam walked away, his footsteps echoing everywhere. I noticed a plaque at the top of the main window: *Intake.*

Intake? What did that mean?

Curious, I approached the window and peeked inside.

No one.

What was going on?

Sighing, I turned around and sat in a chair

as Adam had instructed me to do. Right then, a girl with a messy blond ponytail and huge oval glasses came running from across the room. She held some sort of wooden platform in one hand, and waved the other above her head as if trying to get my attention.

She already had my attention.

"Oh, hi there! S-s-sorry! I had to use the washroom. Coming! Coming!"

Her sneakers squeaked as she ran across the cold, shiny floor. Rather than coming up to me, she ran into the intake area. The door slammed shut behind her and shook the windows.

She reappeared at the front window, grinning from ear to ear, revealing a medium-sized gap between her two front teeth. "Hi!"

I looked around, wondering what she was so excited about. When I didn't find anything interesting, I stood up and approached the window.

Pinned to her pink dress was a little white rectangle that read: Alice.

"Oh, um, hi... Alice."

"You're a Wild Child," she said, matter-of-factly.

"Wild Child?" I asked.

She stuck out her unnaturally red lips. "It means newbie."

Newbie? What did *that* mean?

"Oh," I said.

With that same smile still stretching her face, she turned to something similar to what Adam had been holding, only this one sat firmly in place. She poked at it, as Adam had done.

I was too curious to bite my tongue. Sticking my head inside the open window, I said, "What is that?"

"Oh, this?" She reached for the bright gadget and turned it toward me.

The moment the light hit my eyes, I immediately pulled away. It was overly bright and felt unnatural. My reaction made her laugh.

"This is a computer. And this right here, that's called a screen. Don't worry. You'll get used to the technological lingo around here."

A computer? So that's what Grandma had told me about. That, and the internet, which still didn't make any sense to me. And what had she meant by I'd "get used to it"? Did that mean they intended to keep me here permanently?

I took a step backward, my heart racing.

"Oh, honey," she said. "Don't try it. A few people have tried in the past and let me tell you... it'll make the process a whole lot longer and a whole lot more unpleasant. There's no getting out of here. Trust me."

I swallowed hard.

"Then what am I doing here?" I asked.

She leaned forward and dropped her elbows on the bottom of the window's shelf. Her eyes, blue as the screen she'd shown me, looked twice the size of regular human's eyes behind those humongous glasses.

"To be honest, I'm not sure," she whispered. "I already did an intake on the winner the other day. Never heard of there being two winners before."

"There was a tie," I said, not bothering to get into details about my wanting to stay in Lutum.

"Oh!" she squealed, hurting my ears. "That must be it. I guess you're the second winner."

"They said something about President Ka–"

Without warning, she reached across the counter and slapped a finger over my lips. When I froze, she gently removed her finger. "Wild Children don't speak the president's name."

"Why not?" I asked.

Her smile disappeared. "It's part of the rules. There are many rules here." She paused, squinted one eye, and pointed a pen at me.

What was she pointing at?

"What's your name again?" she asked.

"Silver," I said.

"Right! I had your information right here. As I was saying, rules. Lots of them. And the sooner you learn them, the easier things will be for you."

She made this place sound like Lutum.

I'd always thought Olympus was a place of freedom. At least, that was how the Elites made it out to be.

"Could you please step to your left a little?" she asked.

I glanced down at my feet. There weren't any lines drawn on the floor, so I wasn't sure where she wanted me. I took a single step sideways, and this seemed to please her.

"Why so many rules?" I asked.

"It isn't my place to explain everything to you," she said, playing with the pen between her fingers. "That's Ivy's job. She'll be your counselor for the first week."

"Ivy?" I asked.

Alice dropped her pen. "Your counselor. Keep up, girl."

"No, I get that, but—"

"Sorry, intake's done."

"What? What did you even do—"

She picked up her pen, tapped her temple, and pointed it at a small black globe next to the intake sign. Winking, she said, "Sensor got all the information I need. Now, here's your ticket." She reached across the counter and handed me a thin golden ticket made of some sort of metal.

"What's this?" I asked.

Sighing, Alice rested her face into the palm of her hand. "Listen, Silver. If there's one piece of advice I can give you, it's this: don't ask questions, be polite, and do your time. It'll all be worth it in the end."

"Do my time?" I asked.

What was this, prison? How long would I have to do my time? And what did she mean by, "It'll all be worth it in the end"?

Rolling her eyes playfully at me, she said, "What did I just tell you?"

I bowed my head, feeling like an idiot. "Don't ask questions."

"Exactly. Now, head over there to the ticket machine and stick your ticket inside. It'll work its magic and call the train for you."

So this place is magical.

"You'll then be taken directly to the Evaluation Clinic," she continued. "Nurse Natalia will be waiting for you when you get there."

I almost said, *clinic?* but managed to keep my mouth shut.

As I reached for the ticket, Alice placed a hand over mine. She leaned forward, her smile disappearing, and whispered, "It'll get hard at times, but you can do this, okay?"

She seemed genuinely concerned about me, and for a split second, I saw pain in her eyes.

I wanted to ask her what that was all about, but I bit my tongue. She'd whispered for a reason. Forcing a smile, I nodded and pulled away with the ticket in my hand. There wasn't much information on the ticket—not even my name. At the tip of the ticket were black bars similar to those found on the backs of books.

"Thank you, Alice."

Looking sad, she said, "Good luck."

I appreciated her words, as I'd take all the luck I could get.

With a slouched posture, I made my way to the ticket machine and inserted my solid golden ticket. The machine beeped and sucked it up entirely. If I weren't so petrified about what was to come, I would have giggled the moment the ticket was yanked out of my fingers.

At once, its screen lit up and displayed some information.

Silverstasia Blackwood

Age: 17

Height: 5'6

Weight: 134 lbs

The list continued, but before I could read all of my details, a strange whistling sound screeched throughout the room. Vibrations shook the tiles under my feet, and a loud rattling sound approached. I took a step forward, spotting what looked like a metal railroad up ahead. It was deep in the ground, and I had to get close to see it.

I turned toward the noise—it came from the left, far down inside the black tunnel. My heart raced the louder it got. Why was it getting so loud? A sleek metal machine appeared from the darkness, and the rattling slowed down. It was instead replaced by high-pitched whistling as the machine slowed in speed.

Was this a train? I blinked hard, taking it all in. The pictures I'd seen on pages didn't do it justice. This thing was massive and so clean that it sparkled. How had humans constructed something so incredible?

I expected to see someone at the front—a conductor, or whatever it was called. The fact that no one controlled the train spooked me a bit. Was this thing also automatic, like many things in Olympus?

It came to a full stop right in front of me and its side doors swooshed open. The sound made me jump back, and I stared in awe. The air coming from the inside felt warm and inviting.

If the doors could open on their own, would they also close on their own? And if so, was there a time limit? Afraid of being crushed by the doors, I jumped in quickly.

Fancy red chairs decorated the interior of

the vehicle, and around them were smooth metal bars. I assumed they were to hold onto, but I couldn't be sure. I'd never sat inside a train before. Not knowing what to do with myself, I sat in the chair nearest the door, as this made me feel safer.

Across the upper half of the curved metal walls were brightly lit displays of people talking. Some spoke about products, and others, about available activities in Olympus.

"Tennis, basketball, horseback riding..." The list went on.

Out of nowhere, a monotone voice echoed around me.

"Estimated trip duration: three minutes. Arrival gate: twenty-four."

And with that, the train took off.

CHAPTER 9

I held onto the metal bar in front of me, feeling like my heart might climb out of my chest. The speed was so great that I'd slid back into my seat.

It's too fast, I thought.

"S-slow down!" I shouted. "Please."

Although the train shook and vibrated, the feeling wasn't as intense as what I'd felt in the horse carriage. It was the speed that terrified me. Through the windows, dark walls swept by so fast, it looked like a giant blur.

I sealed my eyes tight, wishing it all away.

That same high-pitched sound returned, and the rumbling in my seat seemed to soften. Were we slowing down? Were we arriving? I swallowed hard and rubbed my clammy palms against my pants.

When we came to a complete stop, my head rocked from front to back.

"You have arrived," came that same voice.

She didn't sound human.

I curled my fingers into the cushion of the seat, not wanting to get up. It was a stupid thought—I had nowhere else to go. But I was afraid of what was to come.

"You have arrived," the voice repeated.

I tried to peer through the window to see where I'd arrived, but to my surprise, I couldn't see anything. It was like the windows had gone dark, or like they'd been covered with something.

Squeezing my grip around the seat's metal bar, I pulled myself up. At the same time, something tickled my ankle. A thread? An insect?

I glance down to spot a little piece of paper wavering in the train's warm airflow.

"What's this?" I whispered.

There was something written on it.

I wanted to reach for the paper to see what was on it, but by the way Alice had warned me that escaping was impossible, I had to assume that I was being watched.

I sat back down, my ankle pressed up against the little slip of paper, and dropped my head into my hands. If anyone *was* watching, I wanted them to think I was experiencing some sort of emotional meltdown.

I dropped my right hand near my ankle and snatched the piece of paper. Right before standing, I slipped it into my pant pocket.

"You have arrived," the voice repeated.

I got the feeling the weird lady wouldn't stop until I got off the train, which only confirmed to me that I *was* being watched.

I stepped toward the door, expecting them to open with a swoosh.

But nothing happened.

I waved a hand, hoping some movement might activate whatever sort of magic it was they used around here. Again, nothing.

"Hello?" I said.

Why wasn't anything happening? Had I done something wrong?

Without warning, a loud whistling sound filled the entire machine around me. I swung around with clenched fists, prepared to defend myself, but no one was nearby. Beneath me, little black holes appeared in the floor, and out from them came dark green smoke.

I held my breath, not wanting to breathe it in. But it hurt my lungs to hold my breath, so eventually, I gave into it. And the next thing I knew, everything went black.

"Silverstasia Blackwood," came a breathy voice.

I was afraid to open my eyes. What I wanted most of all was to wake up in Lutum, where I felt safe with Grandma. But deep down, I knew I was still in Olympus.

"Silverstasia," came that same voice.

The sound of a curtain sliding made me peek from beneath my right eyelid. The woman who'd spoken stood tall with an unimpressed look on her face. She had a sunken face, narrow brown eyes, and a nose with uneven nostrils. Her hair, strawberry blond, sat neatly in a bun at the back of her head. She wore a clean, dark green outfit, and at the front of her shirt was a white rectangle that read: Natalia.

Where was I?

I blinked hard, trying to take everything in. Around my wrist was a white band with writing on top. I pulled at it. It felt like paper. Only then did I realize I was no longer wearing my dirty Lutum clothes. Instead, I'd been placed in a blue robe that also felt like paper.

"What... What's going on?" I asked.

"You're at the clinic," she said, matter-of-factly. "I'm Nurse Natalia."

I shifted to the side, and the bed underneath me squeaked like a mouse. But there was another sound, too—metal on metal. I raised my arm, and panic set in. Around my left wrist was a metal clasp tied to a chain. The other end of the chain went somewhere under the bed.

Why was I tied up?

I tugged on the chain, the sound spreading everywhere.

"What's going on? Tell me!" I said.

"Silverstasia—" Natalia tried.

I tugged on the chain again and scowled. "It's Silver."

At the same time, something pinched my arm, on the inside of my elbow. It felt like a bug bite. But there was no bug. Instead, a bloody tube came out of my arm, and my heart skipped a beat.

This time, I kicked my legs on the bed, the frame shaking wildly from side to side. "Let me go!"

"Silver," Natalia hissed.

The anger in her voice was enough to silence me. "If you don't compose yourself, I'll have to sedate you again."

I frowned, wanting nothing more than to scream and demand they release me.

She raised a computer, or whatever it was Alice had called it, and with a stiff finger, punched in information.

"Dr. Bates will be here any minute to give you your results," she said.

"Dr. Bates? What results? Where am I? And—" I paused, remembering the little note I'd tucked away in my pants pocket. "Where are my clothes? I need them. I had—"

Natalia moved in quickly, grabbed my arm,

and tore out the tube. While she did this, she leaned in close to me, her nose almost pressed up against my shoulder. "You need to learn to compose yourself, do you hear me? I've placed your note in the pocket of your new clothes. Read it only once you've returned to your room, in the bathroom."

The bathroom? What was she talking about? I opened my mouth, but she pulled away and placed the bloody tube on a shiny metal cart.

Don't ask questions, I reminded myself.

With the way both Alice and Natalia had whispered, I knew for certain we were being watched and probably listened to. This place was no different from Lutum, only cleaner and fancier.

The curtain swung open and in came a man dressed in the same clean attire as Nurse Natalia, only it was sky blue. Around his neck was a silver gadget fastened to black tubes, and all I wanted to do was ask him what it was. Across the bridge of his nose were shiny, green-rimmed glasses that paired nicely with his unique hair—the top was black, yet his sideburns were silver. I'd never seen anything like it.

Despite the gray in his hair, he didn't look old. His beige skin appeared smooth and silky as if infused with expensive oils I'd never even heard of. He smiled at me as if I were a toddler, then pulled up a rolling stool and sat on it. He rolled his way to the side of my bed and said, "Silverstasia, what a pleasure. And... Oh my. The resemblance is uncanny."

Resemblance?

Keep your mouth shut, Silver.

"Now, let's take a look." He extracted a small computer from his pocket and pushed his glasses up the bridge of his nose. Scratching at the short salt-and-pepper stubble on his face, he hummed a tune I didn't recognize.

"X-rays came through nicely," he said.

X-rays? What in the world were X-rays?

"Bloodwork looks good..." he mumbled to himself.

He pressed something at the top right-hand corner of his computer, then slipped the gadget into a large pocket in his overcoat. "Well, good news, Silver. You've passed medical."

Passed? What did this mean? That I was healthy? And what did they care if I was healthy? Did it determine my eligibility to receive the serum?

"Does this mean that I'll become an Elite now?" I asked, wishing I'd kept my mouth shut.

He smirked as if amused. "Not quite yet. But the good news is that you're a candidate."

A candidate? I didn't want to be a candidate or an Elite. I thought of Grandma, and my throat swelled. I wanted to go home.

"What does that mean, a candidate?" I asked.

Behind Dr. Bates, Nurse Natalia made her eyes pop out and shook her head—something I assumed meant, *Would you stop talking?*

Dr. Bates smiled sweetly at me again. "All in good time, Silver. The important thing right now is that you're fertile, and we can commence insemination immediately."

Insemination? Again, a word I didn't understand.

"What's that?" I blurted.

Though I searched Natalia's eyes, she didn't offer me anything. Instead, she bit her bottom lip and turned away.

"What do you mean *insemination?*" I said. "It would be nice if you explained this to me."

I knew I'd been warned against asking questions, but I couldn't help myself. I needed answers, and I needed them now.

Dr. Bates sighed and removed his glasses. "It's part of your ascension, Silver. Before you leave the clinic, you'll be given a pamphlet clearly explaining—"

"What's a pamphlet?" I shouted. "I don't want one!"

I was getting impatient. It felt like they were speaking a different language.

I tugged hard on my wrists again, shaking

my bed from side to side. "I want to go home! I never asked to be here! What is wrong with you people? Let me go home!"

Dr. Bates glanced sideways at Nurse Natalia and shook his head—a look that said, *I didn't want to have to do this.* The next thing I knew, he was leaning over me and something sharp jabbed me in the neck.

"What—" I said, but everything became blurry and I went back to sleep.

CHAPTER 10

I woke up in the same bed with a dry mouth and a pounding headache.

How long had I been out? I wanted to continue my outburst, but I didn't have the strength. I felt weak, and calm—the opposite of how I wanted to feel in a situation like this. I needed my strength back.

"Good morning," came Natalia's voice.

I didn't see her until she swung my curtain open and stepped inside my confined space. I wanted to be good and to be polite, but I couldn't help my eyes from narrowing on her.

"I warned you to behave," she said sternly.

How could anyone behave in a place like this? In a place where you were put to sleep and medically tested? I didn't want any of this. And worse, I didn't know what any of it was.

My heart quickened again, the monitor next to me making rapid beeping noises.

"Silver—" Nurse Natalia warned.

"Why are you guys doing this?" I asked. "Why am I even here? Why won't you tell me what any of those big words mean? I have the right to know what you're doing to me. Or am I a prisoner here, too?"

She seemed amused by my last words, as if I didn't know anything at all.

"Far from it," she said. "You were requested here."

"By who? The president?" I asked.

At the sound of the word *president*, she took a step toward me like she wanted to cover my mouth before I spoke the president's name. But I didn't. Instead, I glared at her, wanting answers.

"I'm not privy to that information," she said.

I wanted to keep pushing her for more answers, but in came a woman wearing the same outfit as Nurse Natalia. Her little white rectangle read, Anisa. Unlike Natalia, Anisa appeared a bit older—maybe closer to Dr. Bates's age. Her skin was light brown and youthful, yet there was something about her that made me think she'd been around for quite some time. She glanced at me, but only briefly, then turned to Nurse Natalia and stuck her nose out. "Results?"

"Positive," Natalia said.

Anisa plucked a large brown rectangle with paper right out of Natalia's hands and scanned

90

them. "Good... good... Well done." She handed the object back to Natalia and said, "The patient in bed three is ready for her treatment."

Natalia's brows jumped high on her forehead. "Treatment? We gave her one yesterday. With all due respect—"

"And you're giving her another one today. Unless you want to see that girl get a one-way ticket on the train, you'll make sure she's fertile by the end of the week."

With that, the older woman swept out of the curtained room, her shoes slapping the floor.

Nurse Natalia sighed and rubbed at her neck until it became red. A nervous tic?

"Are you okay?" I asked.

It was obvious that Natalia wanted to answer, No, but she composed herself by forcing a smile. "I have work to do. You need to stay here for another"—she raised her wrist and glanced at what appeared to be a watch—"another fifteen minutes. At least until the sedative wears off. I'll be right back."

I stretched my neck to get a glimpse of her watch—I'd always wanted to see one—but she rushed out of the room too fast. As she disappeared, my curtain swung closed.

I should have laid still, staring at the ceiling, but everyone was so secretive around here. If I wanted answers, I'd simply have to find them myself.

I stretched as far as I could, reaching for the curtain with my unbound arm, and pulled it to the side. Natalia slipped into the patient's room next to me, leaving a wide gap momentarily. Right before the curtain swung back closed, I saw something—someone.

Annabelle.

She stared at the ceiling, her eyes dull and colorless. Her skin, once a creamy light brown, looked gray. It was only when she blinked that I knew she was alive. What had they done to her? She'd won the lottery only the other day.

I thought back to Nurse Anisa's words... *Unless you want to see that girl get a one-way ticket on the train, you'll make sure she's fertile by the end of the week.*

Were they injecting her with stuff to try to make her fertile? Was that even possible?

Whatever they were doing, it looked like they were killing her. Maybe that was the reason Nurse Natalia hadn't wanted to give her another dose of the special treatment. But by the sound of Anisa's words, Annabelle was to either receive the treatment, or get a one-way train ticket. I didn't know what that meant, but I intended to find out.

Nurse Natalia returned shortly after to take off the restraint around my wrist. As I rubbed the inflamed skin where the metal had been, she said, "Have a seat in the waiting room and Ivy will come and get you."

"Ivy?" I asked.

I wasn't sure why Alice had tried to warn me against asking questions. All I'd ever done growing up was ask questions. How was one supposed to learn otherwise?

"Your counselor," she said. "Now get dressed and don't forget your pamphlet." She paused and stared at me. "Were you taught to read?"

"I know how to read," I said.

Frowning, I pulled the curtain closed and changed into my new clothes—a white cotton suit with black sleeves and a black horizontal stripe across the chest. What did these colors symbolize? The Elites had worn all white.

I grabbed the *pamphlet*, which looked like nothing more than bunched paper full of writing and images on it, and made my way over to a small room with orange chairs. The room smelled the same as the clinic—like lemons and something strong. Some sort of cleaning solution, maybe? Even though it smelled better than anything in Lutum, it made me nauseous.

I stared at the cover of the pamphlet—a shiny rectangle with a picture of a young woman at the front. Her skin looked so perfect I couldn't help but wonder if she was even a real person. Maybe they'd made this image using their *computers*.

Behind her was a wide space with lush green grass, and behind it, an exquisite body of water in the shape of an oval. Above the woman's head was a title in bold font: Olympus: Earning Your Right to Absolute Freedom.

Earning my right? With my thumbs, I pried the pamphlet apart, but a loud voice exploded in front of me. "Silverstasia!"

My shoulders jerked forward at the sound. I quickly sat up as if I'd been caught doing something wrong.

The young woman marched toward me, her arms swinging dramatically. Her smile, seemingly too big for her face, made me wonder if she'd suffered some sort of trauma. As she walked, the orange bun on her head wiggled from side to side, as did the single curly strand of hair dangling over her right temple.

Was that some sort of style here in Olympus? As funny as it looked, she wore it well. Around her neck was a gold necklace that matched the watch around her wrist. She wasn't thin, but she wasn't overweight, either. She looked healthy, which was something I wasn't used to seeing. Everyone in Lutum was nothing more than skin and bone. Around her eyes was a blue powder that made her green eyes look bright, and across her lips was something that made her lips look unnaturally red. Was it paint? She wore a blue floral dress with white stripes throughout, and cute matching shoes. Around her waist was a brown leather belt that accentuated her curvy figure.

"Come, come," she said, waving a hand.

With the pamphlet pressed against my chest, I stood and followed her out of the clinic.

"Stinks in there, doesn't it?" she said the moment we walked out.

She was so casual and straightforward that I wasn't sure how to respond.

"I'm Ivy, but you can call me"—she flicked her wrist and giggled—"Ivy."

Why was she being so friendly? Everyone else had behaved so cold and dreary around me. What did she have to be so excited about? She led me down white-floored corridors with matching walls. Every few meters was a solid black door that looked like it didn't belong.

"Where are we going?" I asked.

She leaned into me as we walked, her shoulder touching mine. "To your room, silly."

We went on for what felt like an eternity until we ultimately made a right turn. Everything was so white and blended that I hadn't even realized the corridor was there. But as we turned the corner, something loud broadcasted above our heads.

"Code red. All recruits return to your rooms immediately."

"Uh-oh," Ivy said, though it didn't look like she was all that concerned. In an odd way, she seemed to be enjoying herself. "Come, come, let's get to your room."

Several other people started filling the corridors, their panicked voices climbing the walls like the sound of a thousand flies. Some wore the same outfit as me—a white-and-black uniform—while others wore unique clothing I'd never seen before.

"I don't know, Sari, I've never encountered this before," one man said.

"Get to your rooms, hurry!" someone else cried out.

Ivy hurried down the rest of the corridor, bumping into people as she went. I apologized every time I bumped into someone and tried hard not to do it again.

One by one, black doors swept open and people disappeared behind them, emptying the corridor.

"Here we are!" Ivy said. Next to the black door was a small keypad with buttons lit up in green. She pressed several of the buttons, and the door slid sideways, disappearing inside the wall.

My eyes bulged as I searched for the missing door.

"Welcome to your new living quarters," she said.

As I stepped in, the sound of heavy footsteps echoed behind me. Down the corridor came a dozen Defenders with guns held firmly against their chests, but before I could get a better look, Ivy gave me a shove and said, "Ta-ta!"

The door reappeared, sealing me inside the room.

CHAPTER 11

Y ou're late," came a grim voice.

"Maybe she had to get treatments," said a softer one.

I spun on my heels to find five women sitting around a large circular table. Above them hung dusty light, and on the table sat a deck of cards that appeared as old as the ancient war. Maybe it was. Although the five women all looked different, they all wore the same clothes as me—white uniforms with black sleeves and black stripes across their chests, same as mine.

I stepped closer to them. "Where am I?"

The wooden floorboards creaked as I moved. When a large brown rat scurried across my bare foot, I paused.

"You'd better get used to those," came that same grim voice as earlier. "Just like in Lutum."

The woman sat at the far end of the table, facing me. She was pretty, with thick blond eyebrows, a rounded nose, and plump rosy cheeks. When she spoke, everyone's attention was on her. It made me think she was in charge around here, or at least, the most respected. Her hair, a strawberry blond, hung neatly over her shoulders. When I didn't speak, she leaned forward with her palms flat on the table and a shadow darkened the lower half of her round face. "Why are you late?"

"Star—" said the timid woman next to her.

Clearly, *Star* had earned her name due to her personality, likely having been a child who always demanded everyone's attention. She rolled her light eyes and scratched the end of her eyebrow as if irritated at the thought of being nice to a stranger. "We get a new girl every three hundred and sixty-five days, and this one shows up two days late. Why?"

Although her words had been directed at the group of women around her, I knew she was waiting for me to explain. But what was she talking about? Had they been expecting me? Did they count down the days before a new lottery winner came to Olympus?

Everyone twisted their bodies in their chairs to look at me.

I parted my lips, feeling uncomfortable with all the attention on me.

Star impatiently smacked the table and bulged her eyes out at me. "Well, spit it out, new girl!"

"I don't understand what's going on," I said. "I was on some train, then in some clinic. I-I don't know."

Why was my brain so foggy? Was this because of the green gas I'd inhaled? I wanted to give her the information she requested, but instead, I found myself overwhelmed and not knowing where to start.

This seemed to annoy Star. It was like she'd gone through this several times with different new women and had grown sick of it. Exhaling, she rolled her head back until something cracked, then stuck her nose up in the air. "Why aren't you all chipper? New girls come in here all happy about having won the lottery."

"What?" I said. "I didn't win the lottery. There was a tie, and I said I wanted to stay in Lutum."

Several jaws went slack, and one woman even stood up.

"What?" Star said.

"Y-yeah, it was a tie. This girl. Annabelle. She was the real winner."

Star glared at me as if I were lying. "Who's Annabelle?"

"The girl who won," I said. "She's in some medical clinic, where I was. She doesn't look good, either. Something about fertility treatments."

Star slammed a fist on the table and two cards flew off. Next to her, the shy woman flinched. The cards floated swiftly through the air before landing face-up on the floor.

At the other end of the table, a red-haired woman pointed at the fallen cards. "Damn it, Star, you weren't supposed to see those."

"Forget the game, Danika. Can't you see something's going on here?" Star stood up, revealing a large round belly. "So they brought you in as a replacement."

"A replacement?" I asked.

"Listen, girlie," she said, reminding me of Mother. "I'm only going to explain this once because you're new, and we've all been in your shoes. The only reason they host the lottery every year is 'cause Elites can't reproduce. Something about a side effect of the serum. And it ain't like it's a lottery either. The whole thing's orchestrated. Hadn't you ever wondered why old people don't make it into the lottery?"

"Star!" hissed the redhead. "You aren't even supposed to know that!"

Star blew air out through her lips. "I don't care if they're listening, Danika. I'm carrying one of their kids. You seriously think I'm goin' anywhere?" She then scoffed as if the Elites were some big joke.

"Don't you want to ascend?" said the shy

one.

Star stared at her, and right when I thought she might lash out at her, she tightened her lips and sat back down. She rested an elbow on the table and dropped her head against a tight fist. "It isn't complicated, girlie. You pay your dues until you're twenty-five. They always take a girl away when she turns twenty-five, and then a new one, like you, comes in. Your ceremony takes place every month when you're ovulating, and you'd better hope you get pregnant. 'Cause a girl who can't breed, well... she doesn't stay a *Breeder* very long."

I swallowed hard. "*Ceremony? Breeder?*"

"It's what you are now," Star said. "It's what we all are. These four popped their products out last month." She pointed at the rest of the women, who stared at the tabletop, looking devastated. "You were a Producer in Lutum, and now you're a Breeder in Olympus. Not much has changed. The only difference is, you'll be giving birth every year, and once you reach twenty-five, you'll be rewarded with eternal life."

No one spoke, and the air became heavy. A *Breeder?* I didn't want to be a Breeder. I was only seventeen. I didn't want to carry a child. A wave of nausea hit me and I swallowed hard. My gut had been right all along. Olympus wasn't some happy kingdom. It was a prison, like Lutum.

I'd been a slave all my life. Who was I to think, even for a moment, that I could become something else?

Danika cleared her throat. "You want to play? We have room for one more."

I avoided eye contact with Star as I approached the table. She was so bold and outspoken that it intimidated me. Quietly, I pulled a chair out, sat down, and inched closer, my chair's legs scratching the concrete floor.

"I'm Danika," said the redhead.

Danika looked to be the youngest, which made me presume she'd won last year's lottery. She was pretty and seemed to be the type to get along with most people, though I imagined she didn't hold back if confronted. Her long hair, an auburn red, sat in a loose ponytail behind her back. It was effortless, fastened right below the neckline, and it suited her nicely. It gave her a rebellious look which I thought was cool. Her eyes, a pretty green, reminded me of Grandma's, only brighter. When I didn't respond, she leaned her petite body forward, her loose-fitted clothing barely moving. "I'm from Division 5."

I frowned. I'd always felt bad for Producers in Division 5. They were responsible for livestock, which meant they spent their days raising animals only to slaughter them.

Grandma used to call me an animal whisperer because of my love and understanding of animals. And it wasn't like I ever got the chance to see many of them—the occasional rat or bird and sometimes mice. I couldn't imagine ever killing one.

I always hoped that one day I'd get to see larger animals, like cows, and pigs, or maybe even a dog.

But then I thought back to Selection Day, smiling at the memory of all the horses that had entered our division.

Danika let out a faint chuckle. "People don't usually smile when I tell them what division I'm from—"

"Oh, sorry," I blurted. "No, I was thinking of something else."

"You know," she continued, "Division 5 isn't as bad as most people think. You get used to it when that's all you've ever known. Ya know?"

"Division 2 was the best. The best," said the woman sitting next to her.

I turned to look at her, and her colorless lips pulled up into an awkward smile. It looked either forced or like she'd lost all strength in her facial muscles. Her dark eyes watched me with curiosity, and I waited, expecting her to introduce herself.

When she didn't, I said, "Division 2. That's meal preparation, right?"

"Yes. That's what I said."

I bit my tongue. She tapped her fingers on the table, lost in thought, then said, "Got to sample stuff all the time. Stuff the Elites ate. But keep your mouth shut, 'cause that's a secret."

Star scoffed. "It ain't a secret if ya keep tellin' the whole world, Asako."

The young woman, Asako, gave Star a nasty look, then faked a smile, revealing poorly maintained teeth. When she caught me looking at her missing canine tooth, she tightened her lips into the shape of a button. "It's rude to stare at people's flaws."

"I wasn't—" I said, but Asako stood up, grabbed a small gray booklet with a pen fastened in its spirals, and moved toward the back of the room, where two rows of beds were lined up against the wall.

"Asako's one of a kind," Danika said. "You'll get used to her. Eventually."

Asako didn't look at me again after that, and every time I sensed her watching me from across the room, she'd look away before I could catch her.

"Hey, new girl," said the woman sitting on the opposite side of Danika. "I'm Dax."

Although Dax had remained almost as quiet as the timid woman next to Star, she didn't look shy. She gave off a strong, silent vibe. She didn't bother trying to force a smile, either. Instead, she sucked on her front teeth, crossed her arms, parted her long legs on either side of her chair, and said, "Division 3."

"Construction," I said, matter-of-factly.

Rather than responding, she nodded, her short brown hair barely moving on her head. Her jaw, chiseled and wide, made her look both feminine and masculine at the same time. Around her deep brown eyes were thick lashes that made her eyes look even darker. Her skin, smooth and dark, looked about as tan as mine. But I got the feeling that her complexion wasn't the result of hours spent under the sun.

Although I couldn't see in detail the shape of her body due to her thick white uniform, I could tell she was toned underneath. Overall, she was bigger than everyone else—taller and broad-shouldered. She uncrossed her arms and sat up straight. "Third year here. If I can give you one piece of advice, it's to bite your tongue and remind yourself that one day, this'll all be over."

For some reason, I got the feeling Dax was the most bitter out of everyone in the room. She didn't make it apparent—it was just a feeling. She seemed the most uncomfortable being a Breeder, as if carrying a child was something her body was never intended for.

When it looked like she had nothing else to

add, I shifted my focus to the next girl at the table—a dark-skinned beauty with eyes aimed at her dry hands. She quickly glanced up at me, but only long enough to catch me staring. Why wasn't she saying anything?

"That's Rose," Danika said. "She doesn't speak."

"Not like she can," Star said bitterly. "Sick pieces of shit cut out her tongue."

I swallowed hard. "Who would do something like that?"

I licked the roof of my mouth, imagining what it might feel like to get your tongue cut out.

"Her people," Star said, her nostrils flaring. "She's from Division 1."

Division 1. I'd heard rumors about this division before, but I'd always thought they were only that—rumors. Grandma had once told me that I was lucky to live in Division 9, and that other divisions weren't so lucky. She'd explained to me that some divisions rejected the idea of education altogether. They went so far as to starve their inquisitive young ones, or cut out the tongues of infants who asked too many questions. Division 1 was known for this, and Division 10 wasn't much better. I'd always thought it had something to do with those two divisions being closest to Olympus. Lutum formed a semicircle around the Elites, and

108

maybe in some messed-up kind of way, those closest to them felt they had more to prove.

Sometimes, I thought maybe Grandma was only telling me this so I'd appreciate the life I had, but now I knew she hadn't exaggerated one bit.

Not wanting to come across as rude, I avoided eye contact with Rose and turned my attention to the last girl who had yet to introduce herself—the timid one. She sat next to Star with her head bowed forward. When I looked at her, her cheeks darkened two shades of red. She tucked her shoulder-length brown hair behind one ear, gave me a crooked smile, and said, "I-I'm Echo."

"Echo," I repeated. "That's a nice name."

She seemed to like this. Slowly, her eyes formed little moons. But before her lips could stretch into a smile, she turned her head sideways, allowing her bangs to fall in her face.

"Echo here is a bit shy," Star said, wrapping an arm around Echo and shaking her. "But don't worry. Once she gets to know you, you won't be able to shut 'er up."

Echo's head bobbled as Star shook her, which seemed to make her even more awkward. Still, it was obvious Star knew how to handle Echo's timid personality, and I was certain that with time, Echo would warm up to me.

When Star let her go, Echo tucked her hair behind her ear again and looked up at me. "W-w-what's your name?"

Like everyone else in the room, Echo was a beautiful young woman. Her hair was a light ash brown hair and her eyes were honey brown. Hundreds of little freckles sat atop her cheeks and across the bridge of her nose, and a few stray ones dotted her bottom lip.

Maybe Star was telling the truth. What if the Elites did orchestrate the lottery in their favor? What if they did seek out the youngest and most physically attractive women for reproduction? It made sense, especially given how attractive the Elites and these women were.

I touched my chest. "I'm Silverstasia," I said. "But everyone calls me Silver."

Danika—the cool-looking redhead—parted her lips as if preparing to welcome me to the group when Star smacked a flat palm on the table and a few more cards went flying into the air. "Well, girls, time for bed. Silver, you get bed number 6." She pointed at the far back corner of the room, where a bed sat against the wall, its crumpled sheet looking like it hadn't been washed in months. "Penelope left us three days ago and she was the one responsible for laundry. You can add that to the list of your chores tomorrow."

"Chores?" I said.

Star scoffed as if I were a waste of skin. "Yeah, chores. You didn't think you'd get to live here for free, did you?"

I stared at the web-infested ceiling, at the dusty light fixtures, and at the concrete floor that looked as dirty as my shoeless feet.

"Your chores are written on your headboard," she said. "That's what you'll be doing 'bout nine months out of a year. You know. When you're not poppin' out a kid. Everyone's got a part to play. House chores get done after your daily work for the Elites, if you have time. But laundry affects all of us, so you'd better make the time."

I glanced at Danika and the others, but they remained silent.

"Oh, and I suggest you sleep with your head under your pillow tonight," she added.

I swallowed hard. Why would anyone do such a thing? I must have made a face. Shaking her head, she said, "It's Asako's Eleutho Ceremony."

Was that supposed to tell me something? What did she mean, her *Eleutho Ceremony*?

When I didn't say anything, Star raised her eyebrows high on her forehead. "She's ovulating, which means the Elites are performing insemination tonight. Asako refuses to drink the tea." She paused and pointed at a small glass on a silver platter. Inside was a green, almost brown liquid. "I highly suggest you drink it when your time comes." Then, she lowered her finger and crossed her arms. "Asako says that any altering substance goes against her beliefs. So they have to tie her down, and she isn't afraid to be vocal about it. So, like I said... You'll want to sleep with a pillow over your head."

My heart raced and a sinking feeling in my stomach made me want to vomit. They tied her down?

"When you have your first Eleutho Ceremony," Star said, "we'll mark it right there on the calendar."

I followed her finger to a small kitchen behind us. It wasn't much, but I was amazed to see real-life appliances. On the small white fridge was a magnetic board with a calendar drawn on it. It appeared to be written with some sort of blank ink, and on certain dates were large red X's with a name scribbled underneath. Most names were higher up, and some of them were all on the same day.

When Star caught me staring, she added, "Most of us tend to land on the same day, ya know, 'cause our cycles have to match up. But these three get a break this time round 'cause they just birthed."

Echo, Dax, and Danika looked relieved.

"Sometimes ya can't sleep 'cause three or more ceremonies are happening at once," she added. "But don't worry. It's only a few times per month."

I'd heard about menstrual cycles syncing before, but it wasn't like I'd ever taken the time to ask the women in my division when they were menstruating. It was a taboo subject in Lutum. Women preferred to pretend they didn't experience ovulation or menstruation. Talk of menstruation led to the topic of reproduction, and women weren't allowed to reproduce unless they were specifically chosen by the Elites to grow our population—something that happened roughly every five years.

"They'll be here soon," Star said, scrambling to gather the cards. "If you need to use the washroom, it's that door right there." She pointed at a partially opened door next to the small kitchen.

Dax reached across the table and helped Star bundle everything up.

As I stood up, my chair screeching under me, Rose reached for my hand. Her dark skin looked black against mine and it felt hot to the touch. She stared intently at me as if trying to communicate with her mind, and though she couldn't speak, I knew precisely what she was telling me: *We're in this together.*

CHAPTER 12

The bedsheets smelled of sweat and salt. I breathed out, staring into the darkness. How would I ever survive this place? Being surrounded by filth didn't bother me. What scared me the most was this *Eleutho Ceremony* the women had spoken about, and the term *insemination*. I got the feeling that meant being penetrated somehow. I'd never experienced this before, and I was so terrified I thought I might throw up.

I wasn't ready for this.

I pressed my back against my headboard and pulled my knees up to my chest. Star went around the room, turning off lights and putting things away. For the most part, everyone remained quiet. Star had mentioned that the ceremony would start any time now, but I wasn't certain how that might happen. Would they come blasting down the door? Would they enter quietly and pretend we weren't here?

I certainly wouldn't make it easy for them.

I thought of Star's words: *Asako refuses to drink the tea. I highly recommend you drink it.*

What had she meant by this? What kind of tea was she referring to? I prayed that by some miracle, Mother would find a way to get me out of here before my time came. Deep down, I knew she couldn't help, but it soothed me to imagine she could.

Without warning, a door unlatched, and a creaking sound filled the room. I immediately dropped on my back and raised the sheet over my body. A dim light spread across the floor, up the wall, and on the ceiling.

I shifted my focus over to Asako, who sat the same way as me, her eyes wide and her arms wrapped firmly around her knees.

Three dark figures wearing clear masks and full-body uniforms entered the room. They dragged behind them a cart full of tools—syringes, medical gloves, and medical masks. When the door closed shut behind them, they all disappeared, as did everyone else in the room.

I stared wide-eyed in the darkness.

Heavy footsteps moved toward the bed. One of the masked figures must have grabbed Asako—she whimpered and the bed shook. They were probably tying her down, but I couldn't be sure.

I wanted to get up and shout at them to stop, but I knew better. My big mouth had already gotten me in trouble, and if I wanted to survive long enough to see Grandma again, I'd have to be careful.

The figures breathed out behind their masks as Asako let out soft moans.

I lay in the darkness, my heart pounding so hard my neck pulsated. How long would this take?

Please, make it stop, I thought.

"Hold her still," came a man's voice.

Asako's cries grew louder, and I threw the pillow over my head.

It blocked out some sound, but not enough for me to sleep.

It wasn't long before the noises stopped, and the sound of footsteps and wheels rolling moved toward the door.

The second they left, I heard Asako roll over and sob into her pillow. Light footsteps rushed across the room, and someone whispered to her, comforting her. I couldn't tell who it was.

I was exhausted. I closed my eyes, breathing in the damp scent of sweat, and replayed the sounds over and over in my mind, my stomach in knots.

Time passed, and my thoughts shifted to Mother. I wondered if her fingers had healed up nicely. Was she worried about me? Or was she happy to be rid of me? Then, I thought of Grandma and my throat swelled.

What I wouldn't give to hug her one last time, I thought.

If only I'd known they were going to take me away, I would have made more of an effort to spend my last moments with her. Was she sad? Was her heart hurting as badly as mine? As these thoughts raced through my mind, I fell in and out of consciousness.

I imagined myself floating up toward the ceiling, through the castle, and far away from here. As I flew past countless Defenders, a faint cry took me by surprise. I stopped midair and searched the space around me but couldn't determine where the sound came from.

It grew louder, sounding like someone was in pain.

Suddenly, my leg kicked the way it always did when I was exhausted and I found myself back in Olympus, lying in a dirty bed with my eyes wide open. How long had I been asleep? I closed my eyes again, hoping to return to my fantasy of escaping this place, when that same cry pulled me from my thoughts.

It was an uncontrollable sob.

Asako, I remembered.

"Shh, it's okay," came Danika's voice. "I've got you."

I liked Danika, and for some odd reason, I

trusted her more than anyone. Maybe it was because of how nice she'd been to me, or maybe subconsciously, she reminded me of a more extroverted version of myself.

"You okay?" someone else asked. Dax, I think.

"She needs to rest," Danika said.

Nearby, Star grumbled something. I knew it was Star because all she did was make sounds indicating her displeasure. "She'll get over it. Now quit talking and get to sleep."

I lay quietly, my eyes aimed at the darkness in front of me. It was so dark that if I'd raised my hand in front of my face, I wouldn't have been able to see it. Although I wasn't afraid of the dark, this spooked me a bit. In Lutum, there was always a bit of light penetrating my bedroom window—even if it was only moonlight. But here, I knew, we were somewhere deep underground. I thought back to being locked in the horse carriage and how it had descended under the castle before arriving at the intake area.

I thought about everything until my head hurt. Next to me, Asako continued to cry into her pillow. She'd go silent for a while and start up again. This continued for what seemed like hours, until finally, I turned onto my side and went back to sleep.

I leaned forward, a tomato vine tickling the skin of my ankle.

"Do you see them?" Grandma asked. She crouched, her small back rounded as she reached for a group of red cherry tomatoes.

Unfortunately, my six-year-old arms weren't long enough.

"I can't reach, Grandma."

She plucked a handful of bright red cherry tomatoes from the bushes and pulled her face out of the green shrubs. With a wide grin, she elevated them to eye level, allowing the sun to shine through. "Beautiful, aren't they?"

I stared, mesmerized. It wasn't often that I got to see color in Lutum, which is why I loved gardening with Grandma so much. She'd point out all the ripe fruits and vegetables before we plucked them from their stems, and she even allowed me to hold some now and then.

"Do you want to taste?" she whispered, her eyes scanning our surroundings.

I hesitated. We weren't allowed to eat what we cultivated.

"No one's looking," she said.

Afraid, I shook my head. "I'm okay, Grandma."

She shrugged and placed the tomatoes into a brown basket by her knees. "Come, there are more over here."

Just as I dropped onto my hands and knees, prepared to enter the tomato bush again, Mother's voice took me by surprise.

"Silverstasia!"

I quickly backed out of the bush with leaves stuck in my hair and glanced up at Mother as she marched toward us.

"What are you doing?" she hissed. "You're old enough to be in your own row! Get over there and pick your own vegetables!"

Several rows down were flat garden beds surrounded by kids, many of them several years older than me. Most parents preferred that their children socialize with other kids and stay out of their way. It must have been because they wanted to earn more points without being distracted. Mother seemed to think that I should be doing what every other child was doing, even though all I wanted was to be with Grandma.

I parted my lips to argue, but she gripped my arm, her fingernails pinching my skin.

"Ow, Mother," I said, but she didn't listen.

"I don't know how many times I have to tell you—" she growled, dragging me through the dirt.

I was small, frail, and didn't stand a chance against Mother. She dragged me past a garden bed surrounded by elderly people, who stared at me with big eyes. Why weren't they helping me?

When we reached the garden bed surrounded by children, Mother tossed me hard into a strawberry bush and I scratched my elbow against a sharp twig. Sucking air through my teeth, I cupped my elbow and held it tight.

The look on Mother's face made me feel like garbage. She glared at me, her nose up in the air and her dark, beady eyes burning holes in my face. We stared at each other for what felt like a long time until Mother blew air out and said, "You're exactly like your father."

"Hey, Silver."

I snapped my eyes open despite the crust attached to them. Where was I? How long had I been sleeping? I licked the roof of my mouth and smacked my chapped lips together.

"Here," Danika said.

She sat at the edge of my bed and handed me a glass of water. I grabbed it and chugged it back. She may have chuckled, but I was gulping too loudly to hear her.

"You see that?" she said, pointing up at a display panel above the main door.

Its digits were blue, reminding me of the computers I'd seen in Olympus. The numbers seemed to be counting backward.

14:59:52

"What is that?" I asked.

"That's how much time you have until we start the day."

I'd seen a nonfunctional clock before, but I'd never actually read time.

"It's about fifteen minutes," she clarified.

Star swept past her and shot us a glance. "Yeah, and you'll need every second of it."

"You'll be entering the Pillars for the first time," Danika said.

"Pillars?" I asked.

She opened her mouth to say something when Dax rushed by her, bumping her shoulder. Why was everyone in such a hurry? Star, Dax, Rose, and even Echo hurried into the bathroom, their heads moving around like snakes in front of the only mirror.

A *mirror*, I suddenly realized.

Dax ran her fingers through her short hair, setting pieces in the right place. Below her, Star brushed her hair with a wooden brush. Rose knelt in front of the bathroom sink and splashed water on her face. Echo, being the most mild-tempered of the bunch, tiptoed her way around everyone, trying to find an opening.

"You're going to be around the Prototypes, and trust me, you don't want to give them any excuse to stare at you more than they already do."

"Prototypes?" I repeated.

Danika's eyes shot at the clock and her features hardened. It was obvious she was torn between taking the time to explain to me how the day was going to play out and getting ready with the others.

"They're the children born and raised in Olympus. The ones we create." Her eyes shot up again. "We don't have much time." She reached for my messy hair and twirled it in between her fingers. "Let's get these knots out. The girls tend to hog up the bathroom, so I like to use the kitchen sink."

I cleaned my face in the kitchen sink and allowed Danika to help me brush the knots out of my hair. It felt as though only seconds had passed when a high-pitched beep echoed throughout the room. Above the door, the countdown clock read: 00:00:00.

"Out of time," Danika said.

My heart thudded hard against my ribs as we stood in silence.

Why wasn't anyone moving?

Our bedroom door creaked open and in came a shadowed figure.

CHAPTER 13

Her hair looked even more orange than it had when I first met her.

Ivy walked in wearing a different dress that day—a green, black-spotted thing that hung down past her knees.

Without entering the room, she beamed at us—a smile that didn't quite feel genuine—and turned on her heels. "Come along."

She led us down long corridors until we reached a set of elevators. Behind us came more young adults dressed similar to us—white uniforms with black sleeves and a horizontal stripe, only their stripes were red. Why was Ivy the odd one out? And why wasn't everyone else being escorted, like us? Did this have something to do with us being *Breeders*? Around their wrists were bracelets made of silicone or rubber. They looked like watches, only in place of a watch face was a circular gadget with a steady blue light.

Danika leaned into me and whispered, "Prototypes."

When I made eye contact with the nearest *Prototype*, he turned away, his cheeks turning pink. Why were they standing so far away from us? The elevator dinged, and its white glossy doors swept open on both sides.

I stared in awe, trying to understand how it functioned. Was it floating on something?

"It's safe," Danika said.

I hesitated. How safe? Would it move quickly or slowly?

Ivy didn't seem to care that I'd never set foot inside an elevator. Ivy led the way inside, and Danika nudged me to follow. To my surprise, not a single Prototype followed us in despite there being plenty of space for additional bodies.

"Why are they all staring at us?" I asked.

No one responded.

With a bounce in her step, Ivy moved to the elevator's control panel and pressed a large circular button at the bottom that read, *Pillars.*

The box I stood in jerked sideways and my knees buckled. I must have let out a frightened whimper; Danika rubbed my back and said, "It's okay, really."

I could *feel* that we were descending. It was the strangest sensation.

A mechanical sound hummed all around us,

and I searched the walls, the floor, the ceiling.

Butterflies filled my stomach. How could we be going down, anyway? Weren't we already deep underground?

Ivy whistled a tune and tapped her feet against the elevator floor.

I hated this feeling.

Finally, the elevator stopped moving and my knees buckled again.

Another ding echoed, and the doors slid open. With her head held high, Ivy stepped out onto a concrete surface, and we followed closely. The air was even cooler and damper down here.

Shivering, I gazed around the open space. It was massive and foreign-looking with its extremely high walls, giant metal doors, and white overhead lights. Small flying machines hovered all over the place, carrying bags and boxes of various sizes. They hummed as they traveled through the open space, their white lights flickering in the darkness above. Their movements were fast, calculated, and precise, almost as if they'd been trained to travel a certain route.

Below, Prototypes ranging from the ages of roughly thirteen to eighteen moved about frantically, some transporting items and others controlling gadgets and machinery.

"Welcome to Receiving," Ivy said, extending

her arms in some grand gesture.

I couldn't believe what I was seeing. Everything was so... big.

"Receiving," I breathed.

A faint beeping sound caught my attention, and a man's voice shouted, "A bit more!"

He seemed to be guiding a large gray vehicle backward, all the way to a platform, where more Prototypes waited next to boxes and crates.

"All your hard work gets transported by those right there and distributed throughout Olympus," Ivy said, pointing at the gray machine. Was this a *vehicle*? Its wheels were huge—a single one larger than me—and its windows were so black I couldn't see through. At the front sat a person—someone I assumed controlled this large machine—but all I saw was his or her silhouette. They waited patiently as dozens of Prototypes loaded boxes into the rear of the vehicle.

I flinched when the ground beneath our feet trembled. Despite the loud noise and the far-reaching vibrations, no one seemed bothered by it. I turned to Star, who simply pointed her nose toward the front of the warehouse and at the large metal doors. Another thunderous sound filled the space as the doors slid upward, being pulled by something. Chains? The doors curved as they went up, disappearing into the ceiling.

Someone nudged me, forcing my attention back to the ground. Through the door's opening came a lineup of horse-drawn carts—the same carts that typically made their way into our division every morning to gather what we'd cultivated from the day before.

They were always quick about it, and everyone in the division knew to stay far away from them as they loaded the carts. Defenders would stand around them, prepared to kill anyone who dared come too close.

Muscular black horses strode inside, their hooves clacking against the concrete floor. Unlike the horses I'd seen the Elites riding, these had puffy feet, and they were much larger. Another breed?

Around their faces were leather bridles with little flat circles to cover their eyes. Their harnesses were made of the same material, and they seemed to be attached to the carts behind them. They moved gracefully like they knew exactly where to go without being guided.

Each new cart that entered pulled up behind the one ahead of it, until eventually, ten carts in total sat in a perfect row.

Ten carts, ten colonies, I thought.

One of these had come from Division 9—my home. I wondered how many fruits and vegetables had passed through Grandma's hands. The thought comforted me, and I instinctively took a step toward the carts.

Dax stuck a stiff arm out across my chest. She gave me a menacing look that warned me not to try anything stupid.

"Come along," Ivy said, turning to her right.

I followed, my face aimed at the carts.

Grandma, I thought.

All I wanted was to go back home. I imagined myself sneaking inside the cart, or maybe even under it. That way, when they traveled back to Lutum, I'd be reunited with my family.

But I knew the thought was ridiculous. The truth was, I'd never escape this place—at least not underneath a horse-drawn cart. I had to be more strategic about it.

"Silver," came Ivy's voice.

The scowl on her face didn't suit her. She must have realized she wasn't smiling anymore; she pulled her shoulders back and let out an awful chuckle. "You know, we don't tolerate loose cannons around here."

Was she referring to me? We stared at each other for a moment. When I didn't look away, she said, "I certainly hope you girls manage to tame this wild one."

Star's eyes darted my way. "We will."

Ivy led us to the back wall, where Defenders stood tall in front of four glass doors. One by one, Prototypes approached them, pointing their strange bracelets at some sort of computer panel. Every time they did, a white light flickered, and the glass door swept open for them.

Did we need one of *those* to get in? I rubbed at my bare wrist. "How are we supposed to get in?"

Ivy sighed but didn't respond. She led us to the door on the farthest left, above which was a sign that read, *Clothing*, and wiggled her finger at the Defender on watch. "Open up."

I craned my neck to peek at the other doors: *Food, Goods, Services*.

The Defender, whose face I couldn't see behind that face shield, bent his elbow and pressed a button on his forearm. Little lights flickered. What was that? Did he have some sort of controller in his suit?

At once, our glass door opened.

Ivy smiled at him and curtsied.

Dax was the first to walk through, followed by Danika. I stayed at the back of the line, but when a horse neighed behind me, I couldn't help but look.

One by one, the carts moved again, their hooves smacking and clicking against the concrete. They moved closer to us, but only to allow them space to turn. They were huge. It made me feel frail and small, but I still hoped that someday, I might be allowed to touch one.

"Silver!" Star hissed behind me.

But I couldn't look away.

I counted them as they followed the shape of a half-moon, exiting through the large main entrance. As the seventh cart rode by, I waited, excitement coursing through me. Maybe I'd get to see some produce from my division. Something—anything to make me feel close to home.

The seventh cart finished its turn and the agriculture cart, which had to be from Division 9, came around. The young driver directing the horses looked apathetic—bored, even—and sat slouched, his eyelids flat.

I wanted to ask him to tell Grandma that I was okay—that I was alive—but the thought made me feel stupid. This man had no idea who I was, or who Grandma was. Besides, he was an Elite, or maybe a Prototype. He wasn't on my side.

"Silver!" came Star's voice again.

I was about to turn around and follow the rest of my group into this *Clothing* area when something caught my eye. Something... unusual. One of the horse's feet looked like it had been dipped in a reddish-brown liquid. It seemed sticky and didn't match the rest of its shiny black coat. Was that... blood? I needed to know. Without giving any thought to how the others might react, I moved toward the cart and its horse. I must have spooked it; it neighed and tried to move away from me.

"Hey!" shouted a Defender.

The man sitting in the cart frowned as he tried to regain control of his horses. After he did so, he led the animal forward, along with the rest of the moving line.

That was when I saw the rest of it.

But, it couldn't be. Maybe it was beet juice, I lied to myself.

I couldn't believe what I was seeing. I didn't want to.

Unlike the other carts in the lineup, the cart from my division was no longer a light brown. Instead, it was stained with blood from top to bottom.

CHAPTER 14

kicked the air as Dax wrapped her strong arms around me, holding me back.

Defenders quickly gathered, their metal-encased feet clicking hard against the concrete floor as they pointed large black weapons at us.

"Whoa!" Ivy shouted.

She jumped between the Defenders and me and shook a white-knuckled fist at them. "What the hell do you think you're doing? Put those down, now!"

The Defenders exchanged confused glances—their shielded faces moving from side to side—before they did as she'd instructed and lowered their weapons.

"What's the matter with you?" Ivy shouted. Her face, now three times darker than her copper hair, looked like it might blow up in flames. "My father could have your heads for this! Pointing a gun at a Breeder..."

With bulging eyes, she slapped her frilly dress as if trying to rid it of Defender contaminants. Around us, countless Prototypes watched the scene unfold, but no one said anything. They all looked terrified.

I tried to shout out again, but Dax flattened her hand across my mouth. She pulled me in, my back against her chest, and hissed, "You aren't doing yourself any favors. You need to calm down, do you hear me?"

Calm down? How was I supposed to calm down after seeing so much blood on my division's supply cart? Was it human blood? Had Defenders attacked our division? My heart pounded hard against her forearm as I fought to catch my breath. I inhaled slowly through my nostrils, and every time I blew out, the air bounced off Dax's hand and warmed my face.

"Calm down," she repeated.

Even Rose, the girl who couldn't speak, gave me a look that told me I needed to compose myself.

"Could have been wolves," Echo said. She shook her head sideways, allowing a thick strand of caramel brown hair to hide one eye. "It's a well-known fact that wolves hunt in packs, although historically speaking, wolf attacks on humans are rather rare—"

"Echo," Star hissed. She gave her a look that said, *Shut your mouth or I'll shut it for you,* before turning to me. "Echo's right. It was probably an animal attack. With all the livestock we raise in Division 5, it wouldn't be surprising. I've heard rumors about wolves circling that area late at night."

I wanted to argue that I wasn't from Division 5, but there was no point. My argument would only be met with the counterargument that the divisions weren't all that far from one another.

Star's eyes darted between Ivy, me, and the Defenders. She waited, watching the Defenders with such intensity I wondered if she had authority over them. "Are we good?"

Although she was staring at the Defenders, I knew her words had been intended for me.

I nodded, and Dax slowly let me go.

"Good," Star said. "Now let's get inside our Pillar and get to work."

No one spoke after that, but I could sense people watching me. Even Ivy, who I could tell wanted to recite some speech about how unacceptable my behavior was, kept quiet as she led us to a table in the back of another large room. Rows upon rows of tables filled up the empty space, and between the rows, Prototypes of various ages, genders, and skin tones moved from post to post. Some carried materials, and others carried what looked like sewing equipment.

Star led the group behind a white metal counter, where several chairs stood neatly against the wall. She was the first to pull one out and sit down, and the rest followed. Ivy didn't bother explaining to me what my job would be, which led me to believe it would be straightforward.

She gave me a snooty up-and-down look and huffed. "I'll be back at the end of your shift. I expect you to keep your mouth shut until I get back. Can you manage that?"

It was the first time she hadn't smiled at me.

My instinct was to turn to Star, who then turned to Ivy, and said, "We've got this, Ivy, thanks."

Ivy turned around with balls for fists and stormed out of the room.

The moment Ivy was gone, Dax crossed her arms. "You shouldn't have done that." She ran a hand through her short, tangled hair, looking impatient. "If you want to survive here, Silver, you need to learn to control your emotions."

"I-I'm sorry," I said. "But—"

"No," Star cut in. "Just let it go. It's better if you don't talk anymore. Here." She stood and handed me a pile of clean clothes. They smelled new and fresh—a scent I wasn't accustomed to. "We fold and pack. That's it."

It sounded simple—even more simple than gardening in Lutum. And although uninteresting, it wasn't like I had a choice in the matter. The best thing I could do was behave myself if I ever wanted to see Grandma again. So I grabbed the pile and found my station. I couldn't help but wonder if Breeders were assigned this job because it required little physical effort.

As I folded, I glanced sideways at Star's belly. How far along was she? And was she happy about it? I'd always heard that motherhood was the most magical thing a woman could experience. Well, historically speaking. The few pregnant women I'd seen in Lutum didn't seem too keen about bringing a child into this world.

How would I feel about it? I swallowed hard at the thought of a human life growing inside of me.

"That's her," someone whispered.

I shifted my attention to a few rows away from us, where a young, brown-skinned girl no older than fifteen kept pointing my way. What was she whispering about? And why was she looking at me like that?

The boy standing next to her, a spitting image of her, turned away when I caught him looking.

"Stop staring," he told her.

"But that's her, isn't it?" the girl said. "I heard she refused—"

"Elayna, stop it," the boy hissed. "You aren't supposed to talk about it."

When a Defender walked down the row next to them, the girl tightened her lips and went on to sew a pair of pants. Every few seconds, we'd make eye contact with each other. And the more I looked up from my station, the more eyes I seemed to meet.

Why was everyone staring at me?

Danika came close to me and grabbed something from my table. "This is tape," she said. "It's sticky, and you use it to seal the boxes. And Silver, you're the new girl. They always stare at the new girl. You don't have to stare back."

Beside me, Dax scoffed. "Not like this they don't—"

Star nudged her in the ribs and everyone stopped talking.

By midday, my head pounded. I wasn't used to spending so much time under artificial lights. Would I get used to it? I missed the outdoors, and the fresh air. I missed the scent of tomatoes and fresh garden vegetables.

I finished the pile I'd been working on for the last hour and said, "I'm done."

Danika pointed her petite nose toward a table next to our station. "There's more there. Grab another box. But not a big one. They don't want us lifting anything heavy."

I stood up, stretched my legs, and made my way to the strange table she'd pointed at. I ran my fingers along its hard surface. It felt cool, unlike wood, but equally as hard. What was this material, anyway?

Behind me, Danika let out a chuckle. "It's made of *plastic*. They all are." She knocked on our station's table.

I parted my lips to question her but decided against it.

Plastic.

On the plastic table were cardboard boxes neatly piled atop one another, and inside them was messily folded colorful clothing. I grabbed the box nearest to me and turned around, but as I did, something hard hit me in the shoulder and I dropped the box on my toes.

"Ouch!" I said.

"Oh, I'm so sorry," said the boy who'd bumped into me.

His skin, almost translucent white, glistened with sweat. "I-I-I'm so sorry. I didn't mean to. I'm sorry. I shouldn't even have—"

Why was he freaking out? I smiled at him. "Hey, it's okay. It was an accident."

This didn't seem to calm his anxiety.

So I let out a forced laugh, showed him my elbows, and added, "I'm not hurt or anything. I promise. I mean, I'm not so sure how the clothes are doing, but I can ask them."

My lips pulled into a smirk at my own joke, but he didn't smile at all. He didn't think I was funny. If anything, he was mortified. Why? Had I done something?

In an instant, two Defenders came storming toward us and grabbed him by the arms, raising him off the floor. His heels dragged against the concrete surface as they took him away.

"Hey!" I shouted, running after them. "What are you doing? Let him go!"

The boy didn't struggle—he let them take him as if he had been expecting it. He stared wide-eyed at me, veins popping out of his temples. He was terrified. Frozen. Where were they taking him? He hadn't done anything wrong.

As I ran to catch up, the Defenders turned on me, their black shielded faces reflecting the white lights overhead. The tallest of the two held onto the boy, while the second Defender let go of his grip and walked toward me.

I met him halfway.

What was I thinking? Why couldn't I stop myself? Grandma had always called me *Justice Girl* because of this instinct of mine. She'd once said that if I were a superhero from a comic book, I'd go around ensuring that everyone was treated fairly.

It was ingrained in me to want to help

others.

"Where are you taking him?" I asked.

I took one more step, when out from my pocket came the small note I'd found on the train the day before.

The note!

I'd completely forgotten about it.

My heartbeat doubled as if I'd just finished a race. How had I forgotten about the note? I'd gone to sleep with it still in my pocket. What was I thinking? Although I couldn't see the Defender's eyes, I knew he'd seen the piece of paper float through the air and land on the gray floor; his head tilted slightly downward, the black shield over his face darkening as it moved away from the overhead lights.

"Oh, um—" I tried, but he was too quick.

He walked right up to the note and stomped his foot on it.

"What's this?" came his deep, muffled voice.

"Silver!" Star shouted.

Given the circumstances, I'd have expected her voice to sound shrill and panicked. Instead, she came jogging up to me with a huge smile on her face. With a flick of her wrist, she beamed at the Defender. "Silver's new and she hasn't figured out how to reattach tags yet. I'm so sorry."

She moved right up to the Defender, who refused to budge, and pointed at his black, metallic shoe. "Sorry, do you mind?"

Still, he didn't move.

Star seemed aggravated, and with good reason; Defenders weren't known for their kindness or patience. They despised disobedience, and they especially lacked tolerance for any form of secrecy. In their eyes, rules were meant to be followed without question.

Sometimes I wondered if they were even human underneath those face shields.

"Look," Star said, gripping her hips. "I agree that Silver was totally out of line. It's her first day here in the Pillars and she doesn't know the rules yet. We're already running behind on packaging because of her, and if I don't reattach the tag on this shirt"—she raised a pink frilly top—"well, someone upstairs is going to complain, which means Ivy's going to come down hard on all of us. You don't want that, do you? I sure don't."

The Defender reached for a button next to his face shield and pressed it. At once, the shield disappeared, almost as if by magic. Ignoring Star completely, he marched toward me. The second he stepped off the note, Star dropped to her knees to pick it up as if her life depended on it.

I stared in awe, surprised to see the man behind the face shield. Deep folds sat between his thick, unkempt brows as he moved closer. His jaw was abnormally chiseled as if he spent his nights exercising the surrounding muscles. With wide nostrils, he jabbed a black-gloved finger at me. "That was a mistake, do you hear me?"

Despite breathing out hard, his shoulders seemed to expand. It was like he was trying to make himself look bigger.

Macho, was the word Grandma had taught me.

His eyes, two brown slits, refused to look away from me.

"Jason, let's go," said the other Defender.

In the distance, several other guards approached like moths around a flame. It was like they were trying to figure out if this Defender, Jason, needed additional support.

My inner voice told me to look away—to apologize for my behavior—but I couldn't. Ever since I was a kid, I hated the Defenders. All they ever did was spread fear and cause chaos, and I'd always fantasized about one day being able to stand up to them.

I stared at his thick eyebrows and the way their little hairs stuck straight out the more he scowled.

"Jason!"

With nostrils flaring even wider, Jason reached for a button again, and his shiny face shield reappeared. He spun around without saying a word, swaying his arms in an unnatural motion—too far away from his body. Did he think this made him look stronger? It didn't. It made him look stupid.

I hated it when Defenders carried themselves this way.

When he reached the boy, he grabbed him so roughly that the boy cried out in pain.

"Hey!" I started, but Star grabbed me hard by the hair and I winced.

"Shut your trap," she hissed.

"But what are they—"

Her grip was too strong, and the next thing I knew, Dax had me by the arm. The two of them dragged me back to our station and pushed me into the concrete wall. I grunted when my hip caught the sharp edge of a box, but neither Star nor Dax seemed to care.

"Have you lost your mind?" Dax said.

Star's nostrils flapped like little butterfly wings with every heavy breath. "What the hell is this?"

Although she didn't show me the note, she made her eyes go big and aimed them at her clenched fist. When I parted my lips to answer, she said, "Never mind. Don't say anything. Keep your mouth shut, do you hear me?"

I wanted to argue, but with everyone in my group forming a semicircle around me, I felt outnumbered. They all crossed their arms as if prepared to barricade me if I dared try to go after the boy.

"I won't protect you next time," Star said. "You're lucky they didn't drag you along with that boy."

"What are they going to do to him?" I asked.

The women hesitated.

"Everyone knows that touching a Breeder is grounds for capital punishment," she said, matter-of-factly.

"Like... death?" I said.

"Rules are rules, Silver, and with how awful you are at following them, it wouldn't surprise me if you're dead within a week."

CHAPTER 15

Everyone was quiet as we made our way back to our room. Ivy led the way, acting proud as usual with her nose in the air and a strut to her walk.

Was she still upset about this morning? About my freak-out? Or, did someone inform her about today's second incident in the Pillars?

I thought about the boy and my stomach hurt. Had they actually *killed* him? For simply bumping into me?

You're in Olympus, I reminded myself.

The boy hadn't returned after that, even though the Defenders had. I'd spent hours trying to catch a good glimpse of them—trying to see if there was any blood on their uniforms. But I hadn't seen anything.

"You aren't still upset about the measly blood on that filthy cart, are you?" Ivy said.

I squeezed a fist so tight my fingernails dug into my palms. How could she be so heartless? Danika must have seen my body language change; before I could say anything, she touched my shoulder, calming me instantly.

"Fine, don't talk," Ivy said. "Not like you have anything interesting to say. Your days are all the same." Her hateful demeanor changed in an instant, and she grinned. "Did you hear about the new condos being built to the east of Olympus?"

No one spoke.

Ivy flicked her wrist. "Of course you didn't. Well, they're building five-star living accommodations and Daddy says I'll get first pick!"

Her last words came out as more of a squeal than anything. I'd only heard someone refer to their father as *Daddy* once before. Who was this man? He must have been powerful if he had the authority to give Ivy her first pick, whatever that meant.

Not only that, but after watching Ivy threaten the Defenders that morning, I knew she was somehow protected by her father. Why else talk to the Defenders like she was capable of having them punished? She must have been higher up than they were in the social hierarchy.

"Who's next on the list, anyway?" Ivy said.

"Isn't it you, Star?"

Without responding, Star pressed a hand over her large round belly.

"How far along are you now?" Ivy asked. "Seven months? You must be excited to join the Elites."

Star's jaw tightened. "Penelope was excited."

Penelope, I remembered. Star had spoken of her the other day, and about how she'd left right before I joined.

Ivy looked offended by this. She scrunched her nose and stopped walking, causing Rose to bump into Echo—an awkward moment of many apologies.

"Do you have something you'd like to ask me?" Ivy said.

"No," Star said. "I just wish we'd get to see our old friends. I want to know they're happy."

By old friends, I assumed she meant Penelope, as well as any other women who had left the circle of Breeders.

"You know the rules," Ivy said. "No direct interaction with the Elites. You'll get to see them soon enough."

She walked quickly after this, not allowing Star to add anything else to the conversation. When we arrived at our room, Ivy pressed something on the control panel next to our door, then shooed us all inside. She kept her distance, almost as if she found our way of living so repulsive that she didn't even dare breathe the same air as us.

When I looked back at her, she gave me a full up-and-down look. "I'll see you all in the morning. And Silver—if you ever pull a stunt like that again, I'll have to report it."

I nodded.

Report to who? I wondered. *She must not know about the second incident.*

I wondered if the Defenders involved had kept my outburst to themselves. Maybe they were as afraid of getting in trouble as I was.

As the door swept closed, Dax muttered something under her breath. I wanted to ask her to speak up so I could hear what she was saying, but I got the feeling my words might be taken as hostile. Besides, I'd already caused enough trouble for one day.

Rose stepped away from our group and made her way to the beds at the back. Asako joined her without a word, climbed into bed, and faced the wall.

When Star caught me staring, she nudged me. "Don't talk to her, okay? She shuts down for a few days after the ceremony."

I thought back to last night, feeling sick to my stomach. Poor Asako. Did it hurt? I rubbed my belly, wondering what insemination felt like.

Then, I thought of Ivy, and how she strolled around Olympus like everything was fine. Didn't she care that we were suffering? It made me angry. Was her father someone important?

She spoke of her *Daddy* like he was the president himself.

"Lacie, go grab your gloves," the man said.

He looked about as filthy as me with stained clothes, a face covered in fruit smudges, and greasy, white-speckled hair. The little girl standing next to him, no older than five years old, grinned from ear to ear, squealed, then hopped up and down.

In a panic, the man grabbed her firmly by the shoulders. "What did Daddy tell you about showing excitement, honey?"

The tiny brunette looked up at him with large, watery eyes. "It's... it's private."

"That's right," her father said. "Now, go on. Grab your gloves and meet me back here."

Without hopping this time, she bowed her head and walked with arms scissoring at her sides.

Poor kid, I thought. I remembered being her age, and how Mother had oftentimes slapped me across the face for smiling or laughing in the gardens with Grandma. She'd always told me that unless I wanted to end up dead, I'd better learn to stop smiling so much.

Grandma would then wait until we would return home for the evening to tickle me and explain to me that smiling was something every human being was born to do. She'd explained to me that Lutum was a strange world, and that although there were rules to follow, we couldn't allow them to take away our happiness.

The little girl came back with a pair of gardening gloves dangling at her sides.

The father watched her with a proud smirk on his lips. He parted his lips, likely about to call out her name, when two Defenders approached him.

Had they seen the little girl's reaction?

"That's your third infraction this week," one Defender said. "We warned you to keep her in line."

"I-I'm sorry," the man said.

Without warning, the second Defender smashed the back of his gun in the man's face.

The man stumbled sideways, blinked hard, and reached for his jaw.

Shrieking, his daughter ran toward him.

I immediately dropped my basket of squash and ran toward the girl as fast as I could. I could sense one of the Defenders' eyes on me, but I didn't care. He was too busy bullying the man—

he wouldn't come for me. I also knew better than to try to protect the father. When Defenders cornered someone, anyone who tried to be a hero died along with them. But I wouldn't allow the little girl to be in harm's way.

"Lacie!" I called out. "There you are. What are you doing? You're supposed to be on squash duty with me today."

Her head shot sideways when the Defender punched her father in the stomach. He keeled over and coughed.

"Daddy!" Lacie shouted.

With long strides, I managed to reach her before she got too close to him. I scooped her up in my arms, feeling her soft cheek against mine, and turned her away from the scene I knew no one could stop.

"Daddy!" she cried again.

I bounced her on my hip, trying to distract her. "Hey, Lacie, I have a surprise for you."

She stared at me, her lower lip trembling.

"I'll show you," I added.

With every blow the man took, I cringed. The loud smacking and thumping spread throughout the division, but no one dared say a word. I'd seen this man before, and I knew he had a partner. Was she hiding? Crying? Sometimes, partners would run out to try to save their lover, which never ended well. Most of us had learned by now to keep our mouths shut and to mind our own business.

Still bouncing Lacie on my hip, I brought her to Grandma, who stuck her arms out and wiggled her fingers as if to say, *Hurry, hand her over.*

As I handed her over, I heard shuffling nearby. When I turned, I spotted several women lying in the dirt. What were they doing? It looked like they were piled on top of one another. They squirmed and grunted as the woman at the bottom of the pile dug her nails into the dirt. Were they holding her down? It looked like she was trying to crawl her way out from under them.

When she caught me looking, she made her eyes go so big I feared they might fall out.

What were they doing to her?

She jerked sideways, freeing her mouth from a firm hand. As she was about to shout something, another hand appeared and sealed her mouth shut again.

That was when I realized what was going on—this poor woman was the man's lover. She'd tried to go after him, and these women had saved her life.

The pounding and smashing lasted a few more seconds until finally, everything went silent. I turned around one last time to see the man lying in a pool of his own blood, while the two Defenders stood over him, their fists covered in blood.

"No, no!" Grandma burst out.

Little Lacie ran out of the garden, her long hair fluttering in the wind behind her. She hopped sideways as a few adults tried to snatch her up, then tried to run past me. I quickly reached down and scooped her into my arms, but we didn't stop her in time.

With red, swollen eyes, she stared straight ahead at the horrendous scene, her heart pounding hard against my shoulder.

I expected her to start crying or screaming, but she sat still in my arms, staring ahead.

"She's in shock," Grandma said. "Come, let's get her someplace safe."

I joined everyone at the dining room table, wondering if they would play cards again that evening. To my surprise, no one moved. Instead, they sat in silence, Dax leaning back with her legs slightly parted and Danika tapping her fingers on the table. Rose leaned her head on Asako's shoulder, and despite Asako looking like the type of girl who hated to be touched, she seemed to appreciate the gesture.

When I noticed everyone's focus shift to

the room's countdown clock, I followed their gazes.

00:00:03

Three seconds? Until what?

The ceiling overhead split in two and I flinched. I considered pulling my chair away and running to the corner of the room, but no one else moved. They didn't appear anxious at all. Everyone sat calmly as the hanging light shifted over to the side and particles of dust fell onto the table like snowflakes. Then, out from the ceiling came a wooden platform attached to a metal rod of some kind. It descended slowly. Was someone overhead responsible for this, or was it some sort of mechanical contraption?

I sat in awe as it came down, hovering about our heads. Then, the succulent scent of cooked meat and hot potatoes slipped into my nose. I sat up straight, wanting to breathe in more of this delicious food.

The lower the platform came, the more I salivated. The rod continued to lengthen until the platform landed on the table, making a soft knocking noise. A metal clasp detached from the center of the platform and the rod disappeared back into the ceiling with a hissing sound.

Overhead, the ceiling shifted back into place, as did our hanging light.

But I didn't care about trying to understand the technology. All I could focus on was the food under our noses. On a shiny white plate sat juicy red meat—something that looked so delicious and tender it might fall apart if touched. We rarely ate meat in Lutum, and when we did, it never looked this good. It was always dry and pale-looking. Next to the cooked meat were mashed potatoes. I could smell the butter in them, which was something else we rarely had the privilege of eating in Lutum.

These types of ingredients came from the trade carts, which crossed through the divisions weekly. But the carts were typically loaded with only basics from the other divisions, such as agriculture tools, materials, and scraps of meat. On the rare occasion that something special slipped through—like an entire animal, cheese, or butter—there was never enough to share with everyone, and Mother certainly made no effort to obtain these treats.

But I knew the smell.

I closed my eyes and sucked in the creamy scent as saliva pooled under my tongue.

Why wasn't anyone eating?

A woman's voice echoed all around us. "Nutrients."

At once, everyone reached for a small

translucent cup, or bowl, stacked on top of one another at the edge of the platform. I hadn't even noticed the cups—I'd been too busy staring at the food. There were six in total—clear, flimsy-looking containers no larger than the size of my fist. Inside of them were multicolored balls and oval tablets the size of green peas. What were those things?

I watched as the women around me tossed the different colored pieces into their mouths, chugged some water, and swallowed them back. What were they doing?

"Nutrients," came that same voice again.

When I didn't budge, Danika nudged me in the shoulder and widened her eyes at my cup. "Take it."

Take it? Take what? I reached for the cup and jiggled it, causing the little tablets to bounce around. Were these pills? I'd never swallowed a pill in my life.

Danika must have sensed my fear. She leaned in and whispered, "Take one or two at a time, fill your mouth with a lot of water, and swallow everything back."

I followed her instructions, and although it was awkward and even painful at one point, I finished them.

"Eat," the voice then ordered.

I shot a glance toward the ceiling, wondering where the voice was coming from.

Someone was watching us. Star was the first to stand and reach for a large knife at the center of the wood. She cut the meal evenly and served everyone.

Then, she handed us each a fork. It felt cold and heavy in my hand. I'd only ever used wooden cutlery.

I ate fast, barely swallowing the pieces that entered my mouth. It was so delicious that for a moment, I forgot about Olympus, about Mother, and about Grandma. All I cared about were my taste buds exploding in my mouth.

"Try not to eat too fast," Dax said, watching me as if I were a wild animal. She wiped some brown sauce off the corner of her mouth and poked her fork into a piece of tender meat. "Supper's all you get."

That didn't bother me. I'd spent most of my life surviving off one meal a day. I finished my food, even though I felt like my stomach might burst, and dropped my fork into my plate.

When everyone had finished, the overhead latch opened up, and down came that same metal arm again. It wrapped its metal fingers around the platform's center handle and brought the wooden slab back up. Seconds later, everything was gone, and the ceiling was closed again.

"I'll get the cards," Star said.

I stared at her, wondering if she'd ever give

me back my note. I wanted to know what it said. But now, I understood why Star, along with everyone else in this room, avoided talking about the Elites.

We had no freedom, and we were being monitored.

In fact, I felt even more like a prisoner in Olympus than I had in Lutum.

CHAPTER 16

When I woke up the next morning, I lay still for a moment, my eyes closed. Around me, my new friends rushed in every direction, bickering as they prepared themselves for the day.

But I was exhausted. Couldn't I sleep a bit longer?

After a while, I cracked one eye open and aimed it at the countdown clock.

00:07:52

Seven minutes?

I kicked my legs out of bed and hurried into the bathroom to join the others. With everyone huddled in front of the mirror, there was no room for me. But Danika was kind enough to hand me a tube of something called *toothpaste* and told me to use my finger to rub it all over my teeth.

It tasted fresh and minty, like dessert, and I

found myself wanting more of it.

It wasn't long before Ivy met us at the door, ordering us out of our room. As we walked down the corridor and toward the elevators, she kept talking about the new condos and how excited she was to be getting a presidential suite. I had no idea what that meant, but I knew it was important to her.

Grandma had always taught me never to pass judgment on others. She said that people were complex, and everyone was a survivor of one battle or another. I had always liked that lesson.

Therefore, I tried not to judge Ivy, but she rubbed me the wrong way. Something about her screamed the opposite of genuine, and it made me want to block my ears every time she spoke.

The entire way, no one responded to her, but she kept on babbling. It was almost like she enjoyed hearing herself talk. When we passed the receiving warehouse and our Pillar's entrance, she leaned into the Defender and said, "You let me know if this one gives you any trouble."

I didn't bother turning around. I knew she was referring to me. So I kept my mouth shut as the day went on. Occasionally, I watched the Prototypes work, wondering if I'd see the boy again—the one who'd bumped into me. I still couldn't believe that they would take him away to kill him. It must have been a scare tactic to keep people in line.

Right?

I wanted to question Star on it—to get her to admit that the whole capital punishment thing wasn't true—but I knew she'd only tell me to keep my trap shut.

By noon, I felt like my bladder might explode. I left my workstation and made my way over toward the large signs that read, *Washroom.* I was excited to see the interior. Would it also be tiled, like the one in my room? I still couldn't believe I'd sat on a toilet that flushed and had washed my hands under a tap of running water.

But about halfway there, someone grabbed me by the wrist and yanked hard.

I clenched a fist, prepared to take a swing at my attacker when I realized it was Star.

"What are you doing?" she hissed.

What was her problem? Was I not allowed to pee on my own? I must have scowled at her; she gave me a nasty look that said, *Are you seriously giving me attitude right now?*

Star didn't seem like the type of woman who put up with anything. With flared nostrils, she pulled me hard and led me to the washroom. I tried to get out of her grasp, but she wouldn't let go.

"You're hurting me," I said. "Let me go."

Without warning, she opened the washroom door and shoved me inside—a shiny, white-tiled space big enough to fit a dozen people. It smelled fresh and looked cleaner than any space I'd ever seen in Lutum. One large toilet sat in the corner and the sink in the opposite corner.

Although she didn't step inside with me, she held the door with her foot and poked her head in.

"Where did you find it?" she whispered.

"Find what?" I asked.

She made her eyes pop. "You know what I'm talking about."

It took a few seconds for my brain to register what she was referring to.

"Oh," I said. "The no—"

"Don't," she hissed, and I stopped talking. "Don't say the word. Just tell me where you found it."

My focus shifted to her pants pocket. Did she still have it? Had she read it? Judging by the angry look on her face, it was safe to assume that she had read the note.

"It... It was on the train," I said. "When I first got here."

She whipped her head from side to side to see if anyone was walking by, then stuck her head back inside the washroom. "Yeah, right

166

there," she said loudly. She inched inside a bit more. "Yes, that's the flush. That's the sink."

Why was she yelling?

Behind her appeared a Defender's mirrorlike face shield.

"Only one person at a time," he said, matter-of-factly. "Out."

"Oh, sorry—" Star said, playing an airheaded version of herself. "The newbie started her period, and I only wanted to show her how to insert a tampon. You know, because in Lutum, they don't have—"

The Defender waved a hand as if to say, *I didn't ask for an explanation,* and backed away from Star. "Hurry it up and get out."

Star forced a smile. "Of course. I'll be right out."

The second the Defender turned away, she pressed her face hard against the edge of the door. She squeezed into the bathroom a bit more, careful to keep one foot out as if that made a difference. She then reached into her pocket and pulled out the small note. "You found this on the train?"

She made it sound like I was lying about it.

"Yeah, that's what I said." I took the opportunity to snatch it from her fingers and slip it into my pocket.

A loud bang blasted on the other side of the door, and we both flinched. Star pulled her face out of the bathroom to find the same Defender standing with arms crossed over his puffed chest.

"Out," he ordered.

Star nodded and stepped out next to him. But right before the door slammed shut, she said, "Oh, and Silver, don't forget to *flush*."

The moment the door closed, I breathed out hard and reached for the note inside my pocket. Star hadn't seemed too pleased about the message, so I was curious to know what it said. I pried it apart carefully, its edges curling, and stared at the cursive writing in front of me.

Beyond the horizon, a crumbled column will reach the sky.

At the end of the sentence was a long scribble, like a tail attached to the last letter.

I stared at the ceiling. This was the note that Star had gotten all worked up about? What did it even mean? It sounded like a bunch of gibberish to me. Whoever had written it must have been on the train, likely leaving Olympus rather than entering it. A crumbled column? Reaching the sky? I'd never been any good at deciphering code.

As I stared at the beautiful handwriting, trying to put the puzzle pieces together, another blast against the door made my shoulders jerk so violently I almost dropped the note.

"Hurry it up," Star shouted. "Two minutes, maximum."

What was up with all these rules? They were so frustrating. I did as Star had subtly instructed me to do and tossed the note into the toilet. Then, I emptied my bladder and flushed everything together.

No one would ever see that note again, but the words would never leave my mind.

Now, all I needed to do was figure out what they meant.

"Let's go!" Star shouted again. Then, she spoke in a muffled voice. "Yes, I'm sorry. This is only her second day. She's getting used to using a toilet. She'll be right out."

Poor Star. That same Defender must have been hounding her again. Not wanting to get her into trouble, I hurried out as fast as I could. Star immediately locked arms with me, beamed at the Defender standing nearby, and said, "She must have managed to get it inside."

I hadn't the slightest idea what she was talking about, but whatever it was, it made the Defender walk away.

Star's smile didn't fade, which made me rather uncomfortable. It looked forced.

"Put a smile on your face," she said through clenched teeth.

"What? Why?"

She yanked on my elbow and I almost fell

into her.

"Just do it," she said, still smiling.

I did, though it felt unnatural. I'd never been any good at pretending to smile. Grandma had always said I was an honest child, sometimes to a fault. If something bothered me, I wasn't afraid to voice it aloud.

"Did you flush?" she asked, still smiling.

I felt like I was baring my teeth more than anything, but I kept my lips stretched. "Yeah."

"Good," she said. "Hey, we brought up Penelope yesterday. Did I ever tell you we were great friends?"

This was getting freakishly awkward. When my lips flattened, she tugged on my arm, and I bared my teeth again.

"N-no," I said.

She let out a forced laugh and slapped my forearm. "She was great, really. On the days we were allowed to do crafts, she always outshined everyone. Such a creative woman. You should have seen her handwriting. It was so nice."

What was she getting at? And why were we walking so slowly?

"She taught us all how to write in cursive," she said. "She had the most beautiful cursive handwriting. She'd even attach these cute little tails at the end of her sentences."

My fake smile vanished and my stomach

sank.

When we reached our workstation, Star's smile also disappeared, only to be replaced by her usual scowl. She made her way around the white metal tables and joined the other women, who stared at us curiously.

"What's going on?" Dax asked.

Star flicked her wrist. "Bathroom trouble. Isn't that right, Silver?"

I swallowed hard, feeling like I might throw up.

CHAPTER 17

After what Star had told me, I had a hard time focusing on my work.

My whole life, I'd been raised to believe that every year, one lucky person in Lutum was selected and granted eternal life within the walls of Olympus. But now, I knew none of that was true. If Penelope had been sent off on the train, it meant that I, too, would be sent away from here.

What made me even sicker to my stomach was the thought of being used like cattle, only to then be tossed aside. How were they getting away with this? Why was no one standing up?

They didn't know the truth, I realized.

Every time I glanced up at Star, it was like she wasn't even inside her body anymore. She went on to complete her daily tasks that afternoon without speaking to anyone. At one point, Dax—being the cool and collected one of the group—approached Star and asked, "Hey, you all right over here?"

"Not in a talkative mood, Dax," Star said.

She frowned at the clothes she'd been folding and packed them nicely inside a plastic bag.

Would Star ever come around to telling her friends the truth? Was there any point in them knowing? It wasn't like we could do anything about it. Countless Defenders watched us every day, and our regime was so strict that there was no way to strategically plan anything.

When Ivy came to get us after our shift, she appeared wearing a bright red dress with matching shoes and matching lips. Dangling from her neck was a white pearl necklace that shined beneath the industrial lights. She reminded me a bit of Dorothy from that story I'd read—*The Wizard of Oz*. Only she was nothing like that character and instead reminded me of the evil witch.

"What's up with the long faces?" she asked.

We all walked past her without a word.

She rushed by us to lead the group. "You know, it's quite rude that none of you make the effort to talk to me."

"What the hell do you care?" Star said.

Everyone around us, including two Defenders, stopped what they were doing. Ivy slapped her hands on her hips and puffed out her chest. "Excuse me?"

"You heard me," Star said. "You don't give a rat's ass about us—"

"Hey!" shouted a Defender. He stepped forward with a hand hovering over the gun on his belt.

Ivy flicked her wrist at him. "Don't worry, I have this under control."

She stepped so close to Star I thought she might try to kiss her. "Listen here, you little shit. You have no rights in here, do you understand? With a snap of my fingers, I could make you disappear."

Star didn't seem intimidated. Although she didn't respond, she stared at Ivy as if she were nothing more than an annoying child. Sucking her teeth, she raised her chin, forcing Ivy to tilt her head back to maintain eye contact.

"I'm warning you, Star. You'd better pull your shit together if you ever want to meet your unborn child—"

Without warning, Star raised a tight fist, but she didn't have time to take a swing at Ivy's face. Dax caught her arm midair and forced it down.

"What're you doing?" Dax growled, her voice deep and husky. "Cut it out!"

Star yanked her wrist out of Dax's grip and started walking toward the elevators.

Ivy remained calm, looked Star up and

down, and wiped her hands together. "Smart move, Dax." Twirling on her heels, she grinned from ear to ear. "Nothing to see here, people. Get back to work."

Everyone around us hurried back to their duties, and the sound of chaos resumed.

We were taken back to our room in silence, and when we arrived, Ivy didn't bother saying goodbye or wishing us goodnight. She simply closed the door behind us, leaving us standing in awkward silence.

No one spoke for a while until Danika threw her petite arms in the air and said, "What the hell, Star? Have you completely lost your mind?"

"Me?" Star said. She parted her lips like she was about to say something but instead shook her head and scoffed.

I could sense she was frustrated but didn't want to ruin the lives of those she cared about. If she told them the truth, it would devastate them. To ascend and become an Elite was a better belief than the reality of being sent far away on some mysterious train, never to return.

"Star, can I have a word?" I asked.

She hesitated then nodded and jerked her head sideways as if to say, *Over here.*

I followed her to the bed, where she sat down with her forehead in her palms.

"I'm not gonna say anything, if that's what you think," she said.

"Good," I said. "It won't help anyone. I think we should try to figure out what it meant and go from there."

"I know what it meant, Silver." She snapped her head up, her blue eyes fixated on me. She opened her mouth, but only air came out. "I can't talk about it now. All I can tell you is to look up the definition of *column*."

I scrunched my nose at her. I knew what a column was. But it still didn't make any sense to me. Why did Penelope refer to some damaged column? And what was she talking about? Reaching the sky?

Beyond the horizon, a crumbled column will reach the sky.

"Don't overthink it," Star said. "It isn't literal."

I bit my lip, trying to put the pieces together. Beyond the horizon... A crumbled column... Was there some ancient building I didn't know about? Sighing, Star slapped her knees and got up with a swing of her upper body. She rested a hand over her round belly and said, "Are we eating, or what?"

Supper descended from the ceiling as it had done the night before, only this time, it was steaming lentil soup with a fresh loaf of bread. A bowl of soft butter sat next to it, making my mouth water. After supper, Star didn't bother starting up a game of cards. Holding her belly, she went straight to bed.

Once she was out of sight, Danika leaned forward and dropped her elbows on the dining room table. Her hair, a rich red, looked like blood underneath the overhead light. "What's going on, Silver? Is everything okay?"

"It's complicated," I said, which wasn't a lie. I hoped it would be enough to stop them from interrogating me.

Unfortunately, it wasn't.

"Girl, you're a mess," Asako said, looking as unimpressed as usual.

Dax swatted her shoulder, though not hard enough to cause any pain. "Would you lay off? She's new."

"New," Asako ridiculed. "We were all new at one point, too. You didn't see us causing fights with Ivy or the Defenders."

"Silver had nothing to do with the feud between Star and Ivy," Danika said.

"Well, I mean, since Silver's been here—" Echo tried, but Dax smacked the table.

"Would you guys cut it out? She's sitting right here."

I swallowed hard.

"Maybe she shouldn't be," Asako said, matter-of-factly.

Everyone froze, their jaws hanging slack.

I was taken aback when Rose was the one to slam a tiny fist on the table. She glowered at everyone as if trying to fire arrows from her eyes.

Danika watched her intently. "Rose is right. We stick together. That's what we do."

"Yeah, well, she's going to get us all killed," Asako said. "I, for one, don't want anything to do—"

"Would you guys shut the fuck up?" Star shouted. "Silver isn't the one to blame for any of this, trust me."

Her bed squeaked in the distance as she repositioned herself. She then let out a loud huff and pulled the blanket up to her shoulders. "I'm trying to sleep. So if y'all could keep it down..."

Asako, no more convinced than she was only seconds ago, screeched her chair back and stood up. "I'd rather be sleeping, too."

My cheeks warmed as everyone's eyes turned on me. I wanted to say something—try to defend myself—but I couldn't. Yes, I'd messed up over the last few days, but the real problem was Olympus and the Elites. They were the monsters. Why couldn't anyone see that?

I wanted to shake them. It was so obvious. They were being held prisoners and forced to procreate. How were they okay with this? I stared at the wooden table between us, my eyes slowly wandering to everyone's bellies. Soon, they would all have round bellies like Star.

Hadn't they all given birth recently? Weren't they devastated about losing their children? Or, had they gotten used to this? Was the loss worth eternal life?

No wonder Asako was so bitter. Maybe she still felt the pain of losing her children. I wanted to scream at them and tell them to stand up for their rights, but Olympus was no different from Lutum.

We had no rights, and if anyone dared try to take a stand, the Defenders would cut them down.

Everyone knew that, including me.

Rather than lashing out, I clenched my teeth, stood up, and went to my bed. I reached for my pajamas—a black cotton two-piece button-up—but before I could slip out of my day clothes, a thunderous knock shook the bedroom door.

"Silverstasia Blackwood," came an authoritative male voice.

I swallowed hard, debating whether I should approach the door. When I didn't move, Dax stood up from her chair and opened it. She stepped aside and two tall Defenders dressed in black from head to toe entered the room.

180

"You've been requested," said the one on the left.

"Requested?" I asked.

"What's this about?" Dax cut in.

"Mind your business," said the Defender on the right. He tilted his face shield toward Dax—a warning to stand down.

As much as I wanted to argue with them, I didn't want to cause the girls any more trouble than I already had. So I stood without a word and met them at the room's entrance.

With firm grips around my arms, the Defenders spun me around, prepared to take me out.

"Is she gonna come back?" Star asked from the darkness at the back.

The Defenders froze until the one on the left tilted his head slightly. It was a move that made me feel like he wanted an excuse to hurt someone... like he wanted Star to start mouthing off so he could bring her to wherever he was taking me.

A bed creaked, and Star stepped out into the dining area. "You heard me." She crossed her arms. "Are you going to bring her back? Or are you taking her away forever? I think we have the right to know that, at the very least."

The Defender with the tilted head let go of me so abruptly that I fell into the other guard.

"Rights?" His hoarse and monstrous voice

vibrated throughout the room. He turned around and jabbed a finger at Star, almost like he was trying to crush her from a distance. "You have no rights!"

Star flinched and wrapped her sheet around her body more tightly but didn't back down.

"You've made that pretty clear," she said. "We aren't cattle you can—"

The Defender charged forward and the other women screamed. She didn't have time to run or prepare herself for what was to come. The Defender grabbed her by the throat, causing squiggly veins to bulge from her temples, and dragged her to the back of the room.

"Have I made myself clear?" he growled.

"Beren, you idiot! She's pregnant!" shouted the Defender at my side. He fidgeted, likely trying to decide whether or not to get involved.

"Have I made myself clear?" the bully shouted again.

Star nodded, her beet red face moving up and down so fast it looked like she was convulsing.

"Good," Beren said. He shoved her aside, and she fell against the bed frame, her ribs hitting the solid metal.

She squealed in pain, and at once, everyone in the room rushed to her side, except for Dax.

With two solid fists at her side, she took a step toward Beren. Even though she had no armor or weapon, her height and broad shoulders alone made her intimidating.

She glared at Beren, her jaw muscles popping. She knew that attacking him would probably get her killed, so instead, she pointed at him, her chest heaving with every breath. "You just made one hell of a mistake, you fucking idiot."

Beren, still pumped up on adrenaline and testosterone, stared at her from behind the security of his face shield. He clenched and unclenched his fists, probably fantasizing about beating Dax to a pulp. His breathing became rapid and loud, and I wondered if his shield would eventually fog up from it.

Why wasn't he attacking Dax? Was it because she was right? I recalled the young boy who'd been dragged away from inside the Pillar simply for having fallen into me. Would this Defender be punished for having laid a hand on Star? A pregnant Breeder? I hoped so.

They stood facing each other for what felt like minutes until Beren turned away and grabbed me so tightly around the arm I hopped into the air. "Let's go."

CHAPTER 18

"Where are you taking me?" I asked.

Beren dug into my arm as if trying to release his frustration through the tips of his fingers.

"Beren, that's enough," said the other guard.

His grip around my arm loosened and he released an impatient breath behind his mask.

"You don't get to ask questions," he said.

No questions? I had a right to know where they were taking me.

You have no rights, I remembered.

They walked me down the same corridor Ivy led us every morning and up to the elevators. Without a word, both Defenders led me inside, and Beren turned to the control panel to press a button. I expected him to press the lowest button on the panel—the one that led to the Pillars—but instead, he reached for the highest one.

What was going on? Why was I being taken way up into Olympus?

My stomach felt funny as the elevator moved up quickly. For a moment, I thought I might throw up last night's supper, but I managed to keep everything down. I was still getting used to being in an elevator. How long would it take before I stopped bending my knees every time it moved?

When the elevator stopped, a dinging sound came from above, and the doors swept open. Behind them was a corridor similar to the one underground. Everything was white and so shiny that it looked wet.

Even the lights looked white. I did my best to avoid looking at the ceiling—all it did was hurt my head and make me want to run up to a window to see the warmer color of the sun.

With their fingers still wrapped around my arms, the Defenders led me down the corridor, their heavy boots sounding like drums against the floor. We took a left, and then a right, and I wondered: if I ever tried to escape, how would I even know where to go? Everything looked the same.

Eventually, we reached the end of a corridor. At the back were two black metal doors that looked so out of place it was impossible to stop staring at them. On the left door was a shiny plate that read: Mr. Darwin.

Darwin, I thought.

The name brought me back to a few books by Charles Darwin that I'd read in secret. I'd always considered him such a brilliant man. I'd never met a Darwin before. Could this man be his descendant?

Beren reached for a small button next to the door and pressed it hard.

A few seconds later, the doors made a clicking sound. Slowly, the right one opened, and from inside came a smooth, appealing voice. "Please, come in."

When I was led inside, the first thing I noticed—before even looking at this Mr. Darwin man or inspecting the space around me—was the huge rectangular windows that sat on the back wall. Unlike windows in Lutum, these looked like real windows—the kind made out of glass. They reflected a few items from inside the room, but overall, the glass didn't interfere with the scenery.

I took a step toward them, suddenly realizing how high up I was; I couldn't see anything below. It made me weak in the knees. On the horizon sat a large orange sun, preparing to disappear for the evening.

"Let her go," the man ordered.

My eyes shot toward him. He sat with excellent posture in a red leather chair behind a large wooden desk that was so shiny, it reflected the natural light coming through the windows. Leaning into his chair, he grazed his thumb over his lips. It was a gesture that made me think he was deep in thought. His hair, a dark brown like mine, looked wet and fresh. It was combed over from one side of his head, giving him a clean, polished look. He smiled sweetly at me as if he'd known me all my life.

When he shifted his focus to the guards, one of his eyebrows twitched, and his smile vanished instantly. "Thank you, gentlemen. That'll be all."

Beren hesitated. "Sir, the Breeders aren't supposed to be left unattended—"

Mr. Darwin rolled his red leather chair back and stood up, revealing a fancy black suit that looked like it was worth more than all of the divisions combined. A blue tie hung around his neck. I'd read about ties, but I hadn't seen one before and never imagined they could look so nice.

He plucked at the white bands around his wrists like he was trying to readjust them. "I assure you, Silverstasia will be safe under my care."

The Defenders nodded, their masks reflecting the setting sun's orange glow, and exited the room.

When they were gone, Mr. Darwin extended a clean and polished hand toward a red chair similar to his. It sat in front of his desk, waiting for me. "Please, have a seat."

When I didn't respond, his gaze followed mine. "Do you enjoy the sunset, Miss Blackwood?"

I moved a bit closer to the windows. Across the sky were oranges, purples, and pinks. It was the most beautiful thing I'd ever seen. In Lutum, the concrete walls hid this from us.

Mr. Darwin walked right up to the center window, turned to me, and said, "Come closer. Take a look."

Excited, I rushed to the window. A patch of condensation spread in front of my face as I breathed against the glass.

"Extraordinary, isn't it?" he said.

The orange sun looked humongous, and around it were pink and purple clouds decorating the entire sky. It was so beautiful I almost didn't notice Olympus below—a city full of lights, people, and movement—nor the desolate wastelands all around Olympus.

Where was Lutum? I searched the wastelands, hoping to spot its massive concrete walls, but all I saw was destruction—fields upon fields of dirt and leafless trees.

The sight of it caused an ache in my heart, so I turned my attention back to the sun.

"I've never seen a sunset," I admitted.

"Because of the walls," Mr. Darwin said,

matter-of-factly.

Slowly, I turned to look at him. He was clean-shaven and smelled so good that I kept inhaling to smell him—a combination of mint, spices, and flowers. He observed me with his kind green eyes that sat under thick black brows.

"Y-yes," I said. "And curfew."

"Ah, yes, curfew," he said. "I don't miss that."

My heart skipped a beat. "Are you from Lutum?"

He played with those white things around his wrists again and leaned the weight of his body against the window. Instinctively, I reached for him, thinking he was about to fall to his death.

"Don't worry." He knocked a fist against the glass. "It's hard. I won't fall through and it won't shatter. There's a lot for you to learn, Silver, and I'd like to help with that."

Why hadn't he answered me? Who was this man, and what did he want?

"I don't understand why I'm here," I said. "Is this my Eleutho Ceremony?"

"Oh, heavens, no," he said, laughing quietly.

"Then why am I here?"

Mr. Darwin turned away and returned to his chair. He sat down, quietly grazing the top of his desk with his fingertips. "I have a proposition for you, Silver."

A *proposition?*

I blinked.

"A deal. An offer," he clarified.

How could he possibly have a deal for me? It wasn't like I had anything to offer.

I waited, noting all the furniture across the room—a gray sofa with little copper buttons attached to the armrests; a large fur rug the size of my bedroom in Lutum; a dining room table with a dozen chairs around it.

This man had everything.

I had nothing.

He stood up and moved toward a box-shaped machine with a blue light flashing intermittently. "Would you like a coffee, Silver?"

Coffee? I'd never tasted coffee before.

He pressed a button and the machine whistled. More sounds escaped the little gadget—hissing, clicking, and beeping, until at last, out came a dark brown liquid. It flowed into a white ceramic mug sitting at its base, and an unfamiliar yet pleasant smell swept toward me.

"It will be our little secret," he added.

What did he mean, *secret?* Was I not allowed to drink coffee as a Breeder? Probably not, and the last thing I wanted was this man having leverage over me.

"No thank you," I said.

He extracted the mug, a hot wave of steam dancing at the top, and brought it up to his mouth. He took a tiny sip, then let out a satisfied sigh. "Quite unfortunate that coffee isn't offered in Lutum."

What did he care? He seemed to have everything he wanted here in Olympus. He didn't care about the people of Lutum.

"Silver, you're very quiet," he said. "Please, have a seat. All I ask for is a conversation."

Stepping away from the window, I moved toward the red chair he'd pointed at earlier. With some reluctance, I sat down, my gaze never leaving his.

"Why am I here?" I asked.

Eyes wide, he pulled his face back abruptly. "Are you not happy to be in Olympus, Silver?"

I parted my lips, prepared to tell him how awful this place was and how I wished I'd never left Lutum, when he added, "I realize there is an adjustment period, of course. But please, try to keep an open mind. After all, I spent half of my fortune to get you inside these walls."

CHAPTER 19

There was so much I wanted to ask him, but I couldn't bring myself to speak. Why would this man have paid money to get me inside Olympus? It didn't make any sense. I didn't even know him.

Mr. Darwin scooped up his mug of coffee and stood gracefully, his chair barely moving behind him. "Please, allow me to show you something."

Show me something? Why wasn't he explaining himself?

"I promise to answer all of your questions momentarily," he added as if capable of reading my mind.

Frowning at him, I stood and followed him out through the double doors. He walked with his mug of coffee in one hand, and his other tucked behind his back like the gentlemen I'd read about in history books. Every stride he took made him look like he was walking on water.

How was this man so composed?

Was this how Elites behaved? It was a bit frightening.

We took a left turn, and then a right through the empty corridors. Several doors ran along both sides of the walls, and I couldn't help but wonder what lay behind them. One door, specifically, looked larger than the others. It seemed more robust, as if the Elites wanted to ensure no one could ever enter that way unless they had special authorization.

Right when we walked by the thick door, it opened, and a man with a hunched posture, wearing a long white coat, came walking out backward. He shot his head sideways when he sensed us nearby, and immediately slammed his fist on the access panel next to the door.

As the door closed, I peered inside to see what looked like glass cylinder tubes filled with liquid and something else. Something skin-colored. But the door slammed shut before I could figure out what the containers held.

Mr. Darwin, having heard the door close, spun on his heels to find the man in the white coat smiling from ear to ear.

"Mr. Darwin," the man said, his voice freakishly high-pitched. "I-I-I didn't realize you would be out of your office at this time."

Mr. Darwin elevated his chin. "Tell me, Dr.

Bartek. How is the project coming along?"

Doctor?

The doctor's eyes darted between me and Mr. Darwin but remained mostly on me. It was as if he thought he was being asked a trick question. Either that, or he'd spent the last decade secluded from women and no longer knew how to behave in their presence. "G-g-great. Things are progressing, sir."

Mr. Darwin took a sip of his coffee, his gaze never leaving the doctor, which seemed to make Dr. Bartek uncomfortable. Slapping his hands together, the doctor said, "Well, I have some samples I need to collect." He watched me carefully. "Goodbye for now."

Mr. Darwin nodded. "Goodbye, doctor." When the doctor was gone, he added, "Brilliant man, that one. He's going to change everything here in Olympus."

I wasn't sure what he meant, but I thought it best not to start questioning him. At least not until I knew who this man was and what he wanted from me.

We continued in silence.

"Here it is," Mr. Darwin said.

He reached for a keypad full of numbers and pressed several buttons. At once, the door disappeared into the wall, revealing a room so vast that I had to crane my neck to get a good look inside.

"Go on," Mr. Darwin said.

Was this a trap? Would I be locked in here forever? He must have sensed my hesitation. With a warm hand, he tenderly touched my lower back. "Please, don't be afraid. I think you will appreciate this."

Slowly, I stepped inside, holding my breath.

I couldn't believe what I was seeing.

The room was easily the size of a dozen Lutum homes, with rich wooden floors and high ceilings. On the back wall sat giant rectangular windows like those I'd seen in Mr. Darwin's office. Various light fixtures hung throughout the space, each uniquely designed. I'd only ever heard about places like these in my stories, and I always dreamed of one day seeing something like this with my own eyes.

"This is what we call a living room," Mr. Darwin said, aiming an open palm at the space nearest to us.

At its center were two large three-seater sofas made of a red material that looked soft enough to sleep on. It reminded me of that same material I'd seen on the train—the one that looked like it belonged to royalty. Between the sofas was a shaggy gray rug that I imagined using as a bed. It was probably more comfortable than the one I had underground.

"What's a living room?" I asked.

This seemed to amuse him. "Think of it as a

lounging area. When you want to relax."

Relax, I thought. I knew what the word meant, but it was rarely something I did. And how could one possibly relax when they had to work all day, every day?

"That right there is a television." He pointed at a large black rectangle with a matte screen.

I blinked hard, inching closer toward it.

"It will provide you hours of entertainment—any movie that ever existed."

A movie? As in, moving images? Grandma often boasted about television. But how was it possible? And why was he showing me all of this?

"Come," he said, turning away from the television.

I followed him toward a large kitchen with shiny black countertops and beautiful circular lights overhead.

Mr. Darwin knocked on the counter and I flinched. "Marble."

"Marble?" I repeated.

"The counters," he said.

I wasn't sure what difference that made, but by how proud he looked, I assumed marble was something only rich people could afford. Behind the counter were large machines that looked like they were made mostly of metal.

"Are those—" I said.

"Appliances," he said.

He slid his finger along the handle of the tallest appliance. It had two doors and another drawer-like compartment at the bottom. "This right here is a refrigerator. It keeps your food cool. And this"—he pointed at the drawer at the bottom—"is where the freezer is. It will prevent food from spoiling for months."

I'd read about appliances but never imagined seeing one in real life. I wanted to run up to it and open the freezer to feel the cold air.

"You must know a bit about these appliances," he said. "You always did enjoy reading, didn't you, Silver?"

How did he know that? Had he been watching me? Had I been under close observation my entire life? He must have sensed my doubts; his smile returned and he placed his coffee mug on the counter. It made a soft ticking sound.

"I'm sure you are well aware that everyone in Lutum is monitored," he said, matter-of-factly.

It was confusing to hear an Elite speak this way about Lutum. He didn't sound ashamed of it all.

"I had a feeling," I said.

What confused me was how he knew I'd been reading alone in my room. I'd always heard that no one could see us inside our homes. Had I been mistaken? Were cameras hiding everywhere?

"Lutum is the heart of our world, Silver. Without it, we cannot function, which is why it must continue to operate at full capacity."

You mean without anyone fighting back.

He smirked. "You had quite the collection of books. I'm certain you know all about historic revolutions."

I didn't respond. What was he trying to get at? I wasn't an idiot. I knew that Olympus needed us, the people of Lutum, to survive. What I didn't understand was why we were treated like slaves while they lived like gods.

Mr. Darwin made his way toward a white door and reached for its golden handle. Before opening it, he turned his head slightly. "I'm certain you will appreciate this most of all."

As the door opened, more natural light flooded the space. I followed closely, noting another set of windows at the back of the room. They were spotless and shiny as if they were brand new. Not too far from it sat a humongous bed with tall posts around its frame. The mattress was easily the size of my entire room in Lutum, and across it were fancy purple cushions, a thick gold and purple comforter, and countless pillows leaning against a glossy wooden headboard.

Without a word, Mr. Darwin approached a

small desk that sat neatly against the right wall. It was made of yellow wood, and above it was a light with a small silver chain dangling from its bulb.

Mr. Darwin tugged on the chain and the light came on.

He gripped the matching wooden chair tucked under the desk and pulled it out. Unlike the wooden chairs we had in Lutum—or even the ones given to the Breeders—this one had cushions fastened to it, looking more comfortable than any chair I'd ever sat on.

But then, something else caught my attention.

Something that meant more to me than any television, appliance, or comfortable bed ever could.

Several feet away from the desk stood a tall, straight bookcase. It was so large that it would have been impossible to fit it inside of my Lutum bedroom. A dozen or so shelves ran horizontally across the bookcase, and on them were numerous books, with spines of different colors, thicknesses, and heights, many of which I'd never laid eyes on.

Mr. Darwin dragged a finger along several of the spines. "Fiction, history, science, philosophy, medicine. We have it all, Silver. Anything you want to learn can be found printed inside these pages."

I was too excited to speak, so instead, I scanned the spines, reading titles such as, *Vascular Medicine*, *Great Dialogues of Plato*, *Classical Mechanics*, *and Foundations of Inorganic Chemistry*.

He pointed at something, but I was too busy looking over the titles and ignored his momentary interruption.

"This is the return slot," he said.

He stood next to a small metal latch in the wall that looked large enough to fit several books. But what was a *return slot*?

"When you're finished reading a book, you can simply place it in here and the librarian will bring you something new."

Something new? Was he telling me that even after reading all of these books, I could continue to receive new material? I couldn't believe what I was hearing. My heart pounded hard against my chest and for a moment, I wondered if I was dreaming. Was I even awake? Or was I still underground, sleeping in my small bed next to the other Breeders?

Or worse, had I been drugged and brought into the medical unit? Maybe this was a hallucination.

"This could all be yours," he said.

My head spun. I didn't understand. How could a single person be gifted a space like this?

It isn't right, Silver. Countless people are suffering out there. You can't take this.

"In addition to your new living quarters—which, might I also add comes with room service and a personal chef—you will be removed from the Pillars and permitted to focus on obtaining a proper education to become a reputable member of our society."

This didn't make any sense. I'd read Penelope's note. She never became an Elite despite having served seven years as a Breeder for Olympus. Why would I be any different? Why was I so special?

"Is this some sort of test?" I asked.

"Test?" Mr. Darwin repeated. "Heavens, no." He reached for my shoulder—a gentle caress that made me feel warm and comforted. "A father only wants what's best for his daughter."

CHAPTER 20

as the room spinning around me, or had I ingested something rotten?

"Are you all right, Silver?"

I clutched at the bedpost to keep from tumbling over. "You... You expect me to believe you're my father? That's impossible."

"Impossible?" he repeated. "How so?"

I couldn't answer him. The truth was, I had no idea what to believe. My mother never spoke of my father, and every time I'd brought him up, she'd silenced me as if I were discussing something as awful as a new plague.

"Seventeen years ago, your mother and I were permitted to procreate," he said. "We were one of the dozen couples within Division 9 to be given such a blessing. After several months of trying, your mother would not bear fruit, which led to the assumption that one of us was infertile. We were revoked of our reproduction privilege, and it was assigned to someone else. I didn't know at the time that our last attempt had created you."

"That doesn't explain how you're here, in Olympus, and Mother is suffering in Lutum," I said.

I realized that I may have been stepping out of bounds by speaking to him in such a manner, but I didn't care. If he truly *was* my father, he'd abandoned us and deserved to be punished for that.

"The lottery occurred several months after your mother and I split," he said. "As luck would have it, I won." He stared at his knuckles for a moment as if replaying the vivid memory in his mind. "Your mother never forgave me for leaving."

I wanted to say something along the lines of, *What the hell would you know about Mother? You've been living a life of luxury, entirely oblivious to the suffering around you,* but I realized that getting angry with Mr. Darwin wouldn't do me any favors. The least I could do was hear him out.

He ran a hand over his silky black hair and sat at the edge of the bed, his long legs looking out of place in front of him. "Like you, I was a Breeder when I arrived here."

For a split second, I saw a man from Lutum—a sad man wanting nothing more than to live a life of freedom. But as I stared at him—

his expensive suit, his bright blue tie, his polished leather shoes, and his clean-shaven face—I remembered exactly who this man was.

An Elite.

He breathed out slowly and looked up at me. "You're not a fool, Silver. You know what happens after a Breeder has served their purpose."

My heart skipped a beat. How did he know what I *knew*? I considered arguing with him to try to convince him that I knew nothing about that, but I decided against it. Maybe it was better to let him do the talking.

He wiggled his finger at me and smirked, almost as if capable of seeing my brain firing in every direction. "You're likely wondering why I'm telling you this."

That was exactly what I was wondering, though I didn't vocalize it.

"Like you, Silver, I enjoyed reading while in Lutum." He paused, then added, "Male Breeders and female Breeders lead different lives. Men are given more... freedom."

I bit my tongue, and he continued. "I read so much that a year before I turned twenty-five, I provided invaluable feedback to one of our doctors here in Olympus. Information that would ultimately lead to a discovery."

"What discovery?" I asked.

He slapped his knee. "Ah, I'm afraid I can't

go into details quite yet. At least, not until I'm certain you can be trusted."

"So, what?" I said. "You were offered the serum to stay here in Olympus?"

He nodded. "Precisely. And I have spent the last decade making a name for myself. Building a career, and a fortune, as I watched you grow up in Lutum."

"A fortune you used to get me here? What am I, some prize? You paid to bring me in? This doesn't make any sense!" I let go of the bedpost and started pacing in front of him. "I didn't want to come here. You forced me. Don't you see that? I'm as much a prisoner here as I was in Lutum!"

I wiped my clammy palms together and clenched my teeth.

Calm down, Silver.

He didn't say anything, probably waiting for the storm to pass, but it wasn't over—at least not yet.

"You're lying," I went off again. "I don't believe a word of it."

"What don't you believe, Silver? That I brought you here? That I'm your father? That a Breeder such as myself could become a reputable member of society here in Olympus? Why do you think your name was drawn during the lottery? Your grandmother might believe she had something to do with that, but I specifically requested that you win this year."

I scoffed. "Right. Because you can control where that diamond lands. It's random. The lottery is supposed to be random!"

He bowed his head and folded the wrinkles on his pant leg. "The lottery is nothing more than an illusion, Silver. The diamond contains a chip capable of being manipulated. Unfortunately, it isn't always precise, as you well know."

"The tie," I said, matter-of-factly.

He nodded. "An unexpected turn of events. Had you not refused entry into Olympus, the prize would have been given to you, as originally planned."

"I didn't want your stupid prize!" I snapped. "What do you want from me? Why did you bring me here, in this fancy room? Are you trying to bribe me? I want to go home. Please, just send me home—"

Without warning, my throat swelled, and out came hot tears. I dropped my face into my palms and let out an uncontrollable sob. Mr. Darwin immediately stood up and wrapped a strong arm around me.

I didn't know whether to push him away or accept the comfort. I hadn't felt physical touch since arriving at Olympus, and although I didn't trust the man, his touch calmed me.

"Silver, my sweet Silver," he said soothingly.

"I'm terribly sorry about all of this. All I want is for you to be happy."

I pushed myself away from him and wiped my cheeks. "Then send me home."

Breathing out slowly, he said, "I'd very much like this to be your new home."

"Well, I wouldn't!" I shouted.

He clicked his tongue as if I were nothing more than a disobedient toddler. "I don't believe you're in any position to be making demands, Silver."

Fists clenched, I stared at him. "What do you want from me?"

An exaggerated smile split the bottom half of his face. It looked unnatural, as if invisible fingers were hooking his cheeks. "I want us to be a family."

"You're not my family," I growled.

His smile vanished as quickly as it had appeared. "You have one simple choice to make, Silver. You can either return to the Pillars and breed children for the next seven years, after which you will be discarded like nothing more than a candy wrapper. Or, you can live here, studying and learning as I did, until you become of age, at which point I will grant you the serum."

"You're doing all of this because I'm your daughter?"

He cast his gaze at the floor and smirked—

a look that told me he wasn't telling me the whole truth.

"I know about the note, Silver."

The note? *The note.* I swallowed hard.

"The gentleman responsible for monitoring the trains informed me that you'd found something. Of course, I paid him off to earn his silence, though I can't help but wonder... What did that note say?" He tapped his chin and took a step toward me. "Whatever was written on that slip of paper was enough to cause quite the stir-up among our oldest Breeder, Star, wouldn't you say?"

I thought of Star and how she'd mouthed off to both Ivy and a Defender.

"Star is pregnant," he said. "You do understand that, don't you? She's meant to deliver that child in a few months' time, and children are such a rare commodity that we cannot afford to lose a single one. At least not until—" His voice cut out and he gazed absentmindedly at the wall.

"What's your point?" I said.

"That child is already reserved for a family," he said. "A family who has paid quite a fortune to reserve their Prototype."

"Yeah, another slave," I said. "I know about the Prototypes. They're the same children we breed."

My accusations didn't seem to bother him.

If anything, he looked pleased about it.

"Not a slave," he said. "Contributors. Children are assigned to the workforce at the age of thirteen. They work throughout all of Olympus, providing services to the Elites until they turn eighteen. At that point, they become students and are allowed to choose a profession of interest. They work alongside specialists in their field, learning everything they can. And of course, once they turn twenty-five, they ascend and become reputable members of our society."

Ascend, I remembered. It was another way of saying someone could receive the serum.

I rubbed my temples, trying to absorb all this information.

"What do you want from me?" I said.

"I need you to right your wrongs," he said plainly. "You've stirred up quite a mess ever since you rejected the idea of becoming an Elite. Both for the people of Lutum and Olympus. You've given them a false sense of freedom—of hope, even. Do you understand how dangerous that is? If people begin to take a stand, countless innocent lives will be lost. I need you to return to the Pillars and be a good little girl until Star delivers the child. Keep her calm and see to it that whatever information the both of you have obtained is not shared with the other Breeders."

"I don't understand," I said. "If all you need is to ensure her baby comes out healthy, why not move her to the medical clinic or isolate her from everyone else? That way, she won't hurt anyone, and your big secret won't get revealed."

He clasped his hands together and tightened his lips. "The care of our Breeders has been the same for decades. They are a symbol of hope and longevity among our Prototypes."

"Is that why you make Breeders work in the Pillars with everyone else?"

He nodded. "If Breeders begin disappearing, it will cause a great deal of confusion and fear, not only among the Prototypes but also among the other Breeders. Furthermore, humans are social creatures, Silver. If we begin isolating the mothers, we risk the lives of their offspring."

I understood what he was getting at. If Star mysteriously disappeared, the other women would start to panic and demand answers. And knowing Star, she wouldn't go easily. The other Breeders would fight back.

I pinched the bridge of my nose when Mr. Darwin reached for my shoulder.

"As a show of good faith," he said, "I will see to it that you do not take part in the Eleutho Ceremony."

CHAPTER 21

This was all too much to take in. Did Mr. Darwin expect me to decide right now?

"Think it over," he said as if reading my mind. "Spend the night here and consider your options. Should you get hungry, there is an intercom next to the refrigerator. You can request anything you'd like."

When I didn't say anything, he added, "An intercom allows you to communicate with others. Simply press the red button."

I nodded.

"And these books," he said, "are all yours to read."

How was I supposed to refuse an offer like that? Maybe I was betraying my friends, but I barely knew those women. Was it selfish of me to want to enjoy a bit of this luxurious life? Maybe. But it would be stupid to walk away from such a generous offer. As Mr. Darwin had so boldly stated, I didn't have much of a choice.

Either I accepted his offer, or I resumed my life as a Breeder, only to be discarded once I reached the age of maturity.

I couldn't move. Deep down, I wanted this.

Mr. Darwin, likely sensing how badly I wanted to spend the night in this room, winked at me. "Enjoy your evening, my dear. I will have someone escort you to the Pillars tomorrow morning. Please do not speak of our encounter or our discussion. I would hate to have to revoke my offer."

"I understand," I said.

The bathroom is right over there—" He pointed to another door inside the bedroom. "Soap, shampoo, everything you need is inside. Feel free to take a hot shower or a bath."

A hot shower? I wasn't even sure what that meant. All I knew were cold baths.

He left the room and closed the door behind him. I imagined this place was also monitored and the doors were locked but didn't want to risk exploring my theory. Mr. Darwin had already been generous enough to allow me to sleep here—in a comfortable bed next to an entire library. We needed to remain on good terms.

Without wasting time, I lunged to my feet and began searching through the countless titles on the wooden shelves. The books all looked brand new. At the top right-hand corner of the bookcase was a book entitled, *Olympus: History and Politics*.

When I pulled it out, its hard cover felt silky against the tips of my fingers. If there was one thing I needed to do above all else, it was learn everything I could about this place. After all, I'd be spending the next couple of years here.

I opened the book, the scent of new pages filling my nostrils. How many times had this book been read? It felt as if it had been printed only for me. I knew it hadn't, but I wasn't used to seeing books in such excellent condition. All the books we had in Lutum were missing pages or ripped in certain areas. Some had even lost their covers.

I climbed onto the bed and pushed a pillow up against the wooden headboard. I bounced up and down, getting a feel for the mattress. It was soft and plush and unlike anything I'd ever lain on before. Bending my knees, I brought the book up against my thighs and read the first page.

The book went on about how Olympus was first established—the invention of the immortality serum—also known as the Ambrosia Serum—and the chaos it caused among the less wealthy. Eventually, it led to civil war, which was the war everyone talked about in Lutum. Grandma had told me all about it, and I'd read a few historical texts, but this book felt official.

Reading over the details of the war made my stomach turn. I still couldn't believe how much power the Elites had back then. The creator of the serum, Dr. Elizabeth Ryskee, became the wealthiest woman in the world.

The idea that one person caused all of this was sickening. She'd priced the serum so high that only celebrities and millionaires could obtain a dose. No wonder the regular citizens became upset.

I continued reading with wide eyes, absorbing all this new information.

Everything Mr. Darwin had told me about the Prototypes and how they were assigned to work between the ages of thirteen and eighteen proved to be true. I swept through page after page until I landed on something that caught my eye.

The word *column*.

But it wasn't about a newspaper column or even a structural column. The sentence read: *Columns upon columns of military personnel were assigned the task of containing mass populations.*

With my mind racing, I dropped the book onto the bed and rushed back to the bookcase, searching for a dictionary.

"Come on," I muttered. I slid my finger across every spine, looking for the word

Dictionary. "There's got to be one somewhere... There you are!"

With the tip of my finger, I grabbed the top of the spine and pulled the thick book out from in between other ones. Standing, I split the book open and searched for the word *column* until I found it.

My eyes scanned the definitions under the word, most of which talked about physical structures or newspaper columns. It wasn't until I reached the last paragraph that I saw it: *military.*

A military column, described as a formation of soldiers marching together.

Beyond the horizon, a crumbled column will reach the sky.

That was it. Penelope wasn't talking about some crumbled column at all. She'd written in code. The column she spoke of referred to an army—a rebellion—preparing to stand up against the Elites.

I breathed in sharply to catch my breath. Was it true? And if so, how did Penelope know she'd survive the train ride? What if the Elites simply murdered everyone they transported by train?

I wanted more answers but knew I wouldn't find them, especially not in these books. They were meant to fill my mind with useful knowledge and basic facts about Olympus, nothing more.

I went to sleep that evening surrounded by books in my new bed, wondering if Penelope was even alive or if she'd been killed before even having had the chance to fight back.

By morning, a pleasant bell echoed in the distance. At first, I thought it was part of my dream, but as it grew louder, I realized it wasn't. I shot upright in my bed, more refreshed than I'd ever felt in my life, and rushed to the bedroom door.

"Hello?" I asked.

"Miss Blackwood?" came a sweet, feminine voice.

I craned my neck back to spot a strange surface next to the door. It was black and appeared to have thousands of little holes. The intercom, I remembered. As instructed by Mr. Darwin, I pressed the small red button and said, "H-h-hello?"

It felt weird, yet it intrigued me.

Through the holey surface came that same voice again. "Good morning, Miss Blackwood. My name is Ruliette, and I will be providing your services today."

"Services?" I asked. When she didn't respond, I held the button down again and repeated, "Services?"

"Breakfast, miss," she said.

At once, a screen appeared over the

intercom with vivid images and bold text.

Eggs, pancakes, sausages, muffins, toast.

The list went on.

Breakfast? I thought. I rarely ever ate breakfast in Lutum.

I reached for the button again. "I can choose one thing?" I asked.

"As many as you would like," she said. Her voice sounded so robotic and calculated that I wondered if she was human at all. Maybe I was speaking with a *computer.*

Drool filled my mouth as I stared at the bright images in front of me.

"Um, I'll try everything," I said.

"As you wish, Miss Blackwood."

With that, the room went silent again. I nearly jumped out of my skin when a soft hissing sound echoed from the kitchen. The coffee machine, similar to the one Mr. Darwin had used in his office, lit up and began pouring dark coffee into a blue ceramic mug.

Was someone in here? Or had the machine gone off by itself?

I wasn't sure whether to feel spoiled or frightened.

Was this what life was like as an Elite? Maybe Grandma hadn't been so wrong. Maybe this was a life worth living. I rushed over to the steaming mug, allowing the nutty smell to fill my nostrils. Once it finished pouring the dark liquid, a streak of white liquid was shot into the mug.

Cream? Milk? Grandma often spoke about how much she missed her coffee with cream.

When the lights on the machine turned off, I reached for the cup. It felt hot and inviting in my palms, and I held it up to my chest before tasting it, allowing the hot fumes to warm my neck. I pulled it up to my lips and sipped its surface.

It was unlike anything I'd ever tasted before. As much as I enjoyed the warm temperature in my mouth, I didn't like the taste at all. How could anyone enjoy this? Licking the roof of my mouth, I set the coffee aside.

If I remained here, in this room, would I drink coffee every day? Would the taste grow on me, as I'd so often heard?

Slowly, I made my way over to the tall counter, pulled out a stool, and sat down. The counter felt cold against my skin, unlike the wooden counters in Lutum, which were always warm and filthy.

As I waited for my very first breakfast to arrive, I admired the space around me—everything from the clean floor to the sparkling appliances and even to the warm comfortable air around me. It made me smile, and I found myself wondering, was this happiness? Pleasure? Relaxation? For the first time in my life, I felt content. I wasn't worried about being yelled at, being hungry, or being cold.

It wasn't long before this feeling turned to guilt. What was I doing here, anyway? Back home, people were suffering... being beaten and forced to work despite aching backs, joints, and muscles. Yet, here I was, waiting to be served breakfast that could have easily fed over a dozen people.

I stared at the coffee mug on the counter, wondering how many hands the beans had passed through before being taken out of Lutum and given to the Elites to enjoy.

Would you stop it? I told myself. *You deserve a moment of happiness. Enjoy it before it's gone.*

I did precisely that until that same sweet-sounding bell echoed next to the door.

"May I come in, Miss Blackwood?"

I lunged off my stool and rushed to the door. "Um, y-yes, come in, please."

The door opened smoothly and in came a young woman—no older than me—pushing a silver cart on wheels. She had light brown hair, though it was impossible to tell its length as it remained tucked underneath a small white cap on her head. Her clothes, also white, hung loosely on her petite frame. With a straight back and overly practiced smile, she wheeled the cart inside. On it were silver dome-shaped lids with golden handles. With a pale white hand, she removed each lid, instantly filling the room with smells that made my mouth water.

I stared in awe at all the food before me: fried eggs, crispy toasts piled next to small glass jars of jam, greasy steaming sausages, golden-baked muffins, and fluffy pancakes that looked like they could be used as pillows.

"This... This is all for me?"

Still smiling, she nodded and turned away, prepared to leave the room.

"Wait," I said.

She froze.

"Won't you join me?" I said. "This is way too much food for one person."

Slowly, she turned around. "We only prepare the food, Miss Blackwood."

"You can call me Silver."

She bowed her head respectfully and said, "Silver."

"I'm never going to eat all of this." I picked up a fork and stabbed it into one of the eggs. "I spoke out of excitement earlier. But I don't want there to be any waste."

Her eyes darted at the food.

"Oh," I said, realizing something. "You must eat this all the time, so you must be sick of it."

She licked her lips and stiffened. "I've taste tested a few things," she admitted. "But we aren't allowed to consume what we prepare."

I did a double take. *Unbelievable.* This poor

girl was exactly like us in Lutum. She served only one purpose—to support those around her.

Ruliette took a step forward, prepared to reach for a piece of bacon when a robotic voice blared out of the intercom. "Please prepare to descend into your living quarters in five minutes."

I froze, fried egg wiggling on my fork midair. "Was she talking to me?"

Ruliette retreated, placing her hand inside her pocket. "I believe so, Miss Blackwood. Mr. Darwin has asked that you return to the Pillars today to avoid suspicion."

Suspicion, I thought. I hated that word. Suspicion meant there was something to hide, which in this case, I knew there was. I'd been offered a deal, and the other women weren't allowed to know about it.

Nodding, I shoved as much egg as I could into my mouth, then added a crispy piece of bacon, squishing it past a piece of egg. I drooled as I chewed, not wanting the celebration in my mouth to end. I must have rolled my eyes with pleasure; Ruliette chuckled—a soft, innocent laugh—and turned away when I looked at her.

"I-I'm sorry," I said, my mouth full. "I've never eaten bacon b-before." I swallowed. "And eggs like this... I mean, wow." I stabbed my fork into the pile of hot, steaming yellow stuff. "The only breakfast I've ever had in Lutum was porridge."

"We sometimes feed that to the pigs," Ruliette said. But the moment we made eye contact, she shook her head apologetically and turned away again. "I-I'm sorry."

This time, I shoved hot buttered toast into my mouth. I was enjoying all these tastes so much that I didn't care what Ruliette was saying. She could have called me a pig, for all I cared. All that mattered was my tongue, and the incredible signals it was sending to my brain.

Then, a bell rang at the door, and it slowly opened. Ruliette grabbed the cart and walked backward, leaving me alone in the room.

"It... it was nice to meet you," I called out.

She didn't respond. She probably wasn't allowed to.

From the outside hall came a Defender, his shiny black uniform looking freshly washed. He didn't say a word, but he didn't need to. I knew I had to follow him. Glancing back one last time at the vast room, I admired the high ceilings, the lingering smell of breakfast, and the sparkling wooden floors.

Would I ever see this place again?

CHAPTER 22

"Where were you?" Ivy asked as I stepped out of the elevators, her nose raised slightly higher than usual.

"Um, testing," I said.

"Testing?" she repeated.

"Yeah, medical testing."

It was obvious by the way she was waiting next to the elevator with her arms crossed over her chest that she didn't believe me. Although she didn't know which floor I was coming from, or where I'd spent the night, she knew that I hadn't slept in my usual living quarters.

"I was told to come get you," she said. "You may also want to learn to lie better if you want to convince your friends."

Though I parted my lips to defend myself, she spun around, adjusted her high-waisted skirt, and marched down the hallway. The Defender next to me left down another corridor. As Ivy's shoes ticked against the floor, I followed her to my quarters. She knocked on the door and we waited. Danika was the first to emerge, her green eyes landing on me.

"Silver!" she exclaimed, but Ivy took a step forward, shielding me from Danika.

"Keep it down," Ivy warned.

Danika brushed past her and grabbed my shoulders. "Where were you? We were so worried."

The other girls came out, each one circling me like children around a dead bird.

I shook my head, not wanting to lie to them. Maybe if I refused to speak, they'd leave it alone. But they didn't. Danika's eyes got even bigger as she waited for me to tell them everything.

"Some medical testing," I said.

She pulled her face back, folds appearing everywhere. "What do you mean, *testing*?" She snapped her head sideways and stared at Ivy. "Since when do you guys do testing in the middle of the night?"

Ivy stuck her nose in the air like she always did when someone asked her something she didn't want to answer.

"I'm fine, really," I said.

I felt like a fraud. If the women found out that I'd spent the night in a comfortable bed, contemplating saving my skin despite knowing their futures were all doomed, they'd never forgive me. And why had Mr. Darwin given me those details, anyways? What kind of sick game was he playing? Did he think I'd feel special knowing I'd be the only one saved? Was I supposed to feel special? Because I didn't. I felt awful.

Whatever he had planned, it was risky. He had no way of knowing I wouldn't admit everything to the women. Or, maybe he did—maybe he relied on what every human being had in common—a will to survive.

If I spoke, my future was dark and grim. If I did as he'd instructed, I was promised paradise.

"Hey, you okay?" Danika asked, shaking me from my thoughts.

She stuck a finger in Ivy's face. "You guys had no right taking her like that."

I wanted to tell Danika to stop throwing accusations at Ivy, especially given that she had no idea where I'd spent the night, but I knew it was best to keep my mouth shut.

Ivy made a high-pitched *umph* sound, twirled on her heels, and marched straight for the elevators, her wide hips swaying from side to side.

Dax rolled her eyes and followed, as did everyone else.

The walk to the Pillars was quiet. I could sense curiosity building around me, and all I wanted was for everyone to leave me alone. I wasn't a good liar—I'd never had much reason to lie growing up. The more they asked me, the greater the chance that I would break and tell them everything.

We moved to our station and began our day's work. Every few seconds, someone shifted or looked at me a certain way. It was like they were waiting for me to say, "Okay, so here is what *really* happened."

But every time it seemed like one of the women was about to ask me, a Defender would walk by. The only one who didn't seem curious was Star. She stood in the corner of our station, frowning the entire time. What was she thinking about? The note? Penelope's handwriting? The discovery had messed her up.

She looked defeated, like she'd given up on everything.

Would this knowledge affect the health of her child? I stared at her belly, which sat firmly on her thighs. Her baby was due to arrive any day; upholding my part of the deal wouldn't be difficult to manage. All I had to do was ensure she remained calm until that happened.

Why are you even considering this? You should be telling her the truth. You should be telling everyone the truth.

My own behavior repulsed me.

But the feeling didn't last long. Rapid footsteps rushed toward me and I shot my head up. No one ran in the Pillars. What was going on?

As I finished taping a cardboard box shut, a girl came running straight toward me. I frowned, confused by what was happening, when she launched through the air with bared teeth, her body sliding across the table in front of me. Boxes flew in every direction, as did my roll of tape and a pair of scissors.

I didn't have time to move.

She slid right into me, throwing me to the floor. My head smashed hard against the concrete under me, and before I could realize what had happened, cold hands gripped me by the throat.

"This is your fault!" she shouted.

She shook me violently, causing my head to bounce off the ground again. I didn't feel any pain. Instead, it was more like an out-of-body sensation. I couldn't quite understand what was happening.

I blinked hard, and the woman's angry face came into view—a full set of teeth, wild eyes, and dark pink gums.

"It's your fault!" she shouted again, warm saliva sprinkling my cheeks.

I wanted to say something—ask her what she was talking about—but I couldn't breathe.

My face began to swell and I clawed at her forearms, trying to stop her from strangling me. Why was she doing this? Who was she? I'd never seen her before.

Her chestnut hair dangled on either side of her face, casting a shadow under her already dark eyes. I slapped her arm again, but all it did was cause her to squeeze harder.

She wasn't large by any means; she had a petite frame, her neck easily the size of one of my biceps. But she'd come at me so fast that I hadn't had time to defend myself. My confusion didn't help, either.

Dax grabbed her by the back of her hair and pulled hard. The woman cried out, enraged, and swung a fist at Dax. When she missed, Dax grabbed her by her bony arms and smashed her face-first into one of our plastic folding tables. Two more boxes flew off, along with a pile of clothes, but Dax didn't seem to care. Her muscles bulged through her uniform as she held the woman down.

Two Defenders instantly shoved their way through our thickening crowd, using their plated shoulders to clear a path.

"Out of the way!"

"She attacked—" Dax tried, but the Defenders didn't seem to care what the story was. They shoved Dax aside like she was equally to blame, then grabbed the woman by the arms so roughly it was a wonder her arms didn't snap in half.

"Their blood is on your hands! Do you hear me?" the woman shouted as the Defenders dragged her out of the Pillars. "You did this! You fucking bitch!" Her voice softened as they took her farther and farther away. "You'll pay for this!"

Danika rushed to my side, tucked her red hair behind her ears, and helped me up. She rubbed my shoulders as if trying to warm me, then said, "Hey, you okay?"

I watched the crowd around us. People whispered, some confused and others angry. Why were they all staring at me? What had I done?

I rubbed my throat and swallowed hard, a dull pain spreading into my throat. "I-I don't get it. I didn't do anything. Who was that girl?"

A sweet voice erupted from behind Dax. "That was Clarisse."

Dax moved aside. Behind her stood a young, light-featured boy with fierce blue eyes as bright as the overhead lights. His hair was cut so short he almost looked bald. He blinked hard, maybe a nervous tick, and said, "D-d-division 9. Isn't that where you're from, miss?"

I took a step toward him and nodded.

He turned his head from side to side like he was preparing to tell us some big secret. I got the feeling the only reason he was even talking to us Breeders was because the Defenders had their hands full. "Everyone knows Clarisse. She always talks about how she thinks her birth mom comes from Division 9. We aren't allowed to know who our birth moms are. They don't tell us. B-b-but Clarisse says she's always known. A feeling she couldn't shake." He shrugged, clearly confused by Clarisse's strong opinions. "I don't know. I think she only wants to belong somewhere." He jerked his head sideways. "Smith overheard something... something about a fight in Division 9 a few days ago."

He pointed at a dark-skinned boy who stood at the center of the Pillars, his posture slouched over a sewing machine as he stitched a sleeve together.

My stomach sank. "A fight? What do you mean, a fight?"

"Um, I don't know," the boy said. "A-a-a rebellion or something. After you refused to come here, and after they took you anyways."

My head spun and I swallowed hard, fighting to hold back the bile in my stomach.

The horse carts.

The blood.

It all made sense now.

"They slaughtered them," I breathed, though it didn't even feel like I had spoken; it was as if someone else had taken over my body and I was no longer in control.

"Well, those who tried to fight," the boy said, looking sad. "Apparently it was more than half the division." He paused and bit his thin bottom lip. "I-I-I think Clarisse blames you for that."

CHAPTER 23

G randma," I said.

I hadn't realized I was shoving Dax until she grabbed my shoulders and forced me into a chair.

"There's nothing you can do," she hissed. "Keep your mouth shut and your head low."

"But Grandma—" I tried again.

"Would you give her a break?" Danika said. "She's in shock. It's a lot to take in."

Dax snapped her head sideways at Danika. "I don't care. She needs to fall in line like the rest of us."

"Or what?" Star said. She stood up, holding her belly, and marched her way toward us. Although several inches shorter than Dax, her anger made her look about as intimidating as Dax.

Tilting her head, she came close to Dax. "What are they gonna do? Huh? Kill us?"

It was obvious that Dax didn't know how to

respond to this new version of Star. She opened her mouth, but nothing came out.

"Don't you guys see what's going on?" Star said. "We're objects. Nothing more."

In the background, Asako rolled her eyes and continued folding piles of clothes. Rose and Echo, too, remained quiet.

"Why are you doing this?" Dax said. "You're gonna lose your ascension."

Star scoffed so loudly in her face that several heads turned our way.

"Hey!" shouted a Defender.

Star didn't care. Ignoring him, she jabbed a finger in Dax's chest and said, "Ascension? Why don't you get your head out of your ass and stop believing the bullshit they're feeding you? There is no ascension!"

My heart skipped a beat. How did Mr. Darwin expect me to keep Star under control? That woman wasn't afraid of anyone, and when she had an opinion, she wasn't afraid to voice it. She already knew that the promise of ascension was a lie. How could I convince her otherwise?

"Star—" I tried.

"Shut your trap, Silver," she said.

I was so taken aback that I didn't know what to do. Aside from my mother, no one had ever spoken to me like that. Was this normal behavior in the real world? Mr. Darwin had put his trust in the wrong person.

"It's all bullshit, okay?" Star continued.

"You, back to your post!" a Defender shouted. As he moved toward us, his hand hovered over what appeared to be a baton or an electric weapon.

"Or what, asshole?" Star's face darkened three shades of red.

"Okay!" came a chipper voice. At once, Ivy ran toward Star, her long skirt dragging in the breeze she created. "I think hormones are a little out of whack over here." She forced a smile and grabbed Star by the arm.

"This one is out of line!" the Defender growled. He extracted his baton and aimed it at Star.

"I absolutely agree," Ivy said, "but as you can see"—she showcased Star's belly with an open hand"—this woman is extremely pregnant, and her hormones are all over the place. I will be escorting her to the clinic, if you don't mind—"

"I do mind," the Defender said, tightening his gloved hand around his baton.

I wasn't sure what came over me, but suddenly, I stepped forward, blocking Star from the Defender. Was it my anger? My need to protect the vulnerable? I should have minded my business, but I couldn't help myself. "What are you going to do with that?" I pointed at his baton. "Beat a pregnant woman? Is that how you operate here in Olympus? I thought Olympus was supposed to be a place of happiness... a place where people's dreams came true. But from where I'm standing, it feels like we're in Lutum."

The entire room fell silent.

Although I couldn't see the Defender's face behind his face shield, I imagined him frowning. He probably wasn't used to being talked back to, let alone questioned about Olympus's reputation.

Even Ivy went quiet as I stood with my hands on my hips.

"Get out of my way, little girl," the Defender said.

"I'm not moving," I said. "If you want to beat on me too, go ahead. Show these people what Olympus *really* stands for."

He took a step toward me, but something told me he wasn't sure what he was doing. Maybe it was the way he hesitated, or maybe it was how fast his shoulders were bouncing up and down—rapid breathing no doubt caused by anxiety.

Dax moved next to me. "You want to beat on me, too?"

Next, Danika joined my side. "Or me?"

Rose and Echo joined our human barrier and without a word, crossed their arms over their chests.

All of a sudden, someone from the group of Prototypes shouted, "Baby beater!"

Someone threw a ball of yarn at the Defender's head, and more voices erupted throughout the Pillars.

"Monster!"

"Useless!"

"Pick on someone your own size!"

I couldn't believe what I was seeing. Even the Prototypes—all teenagers born and raised in Olympus—were standing up for us. For the first time in my life, I felt like I belonged... like I was part of something bigger than myself. In Lutum, no one had ever dared stand up to a Defender, and now, hundreds of people had followed my example.

My lips stretched into a smile as the Defender froze.

Before anything else could happen, a loud alarm blared overhead. Red lights flashed as the sound filled the Pillars, and one by one, the Prototypes rushed out of the room.

CHAPTER 24

D o you have any idea what you've done?" Ivy said, out of breath.

She hurried down the corridor, urging us to follow.

"He's going to have my head for this... Oh God. I can't... I can't believe you all did that."

As we ran with the crowd of Prototypes, the alarm continued to sound. People ran in all directions, trying to run back into their living quarters.

Although I'd never heard this alarm before, I knew it wasn't good. What were they going to do? Punish everyone? Were people running to hide? Or was the alarm meant to prompt people to return to their units?

As usual, Ivy didn't follow us inside our room. Instead, she jabbed a stiff finger at all of us. "You'd better be prepared for consequences."

With that, she stormed off.

The moment our door closed, the deafening sound stopped.

Danika was the first to start pacing back and forth. "This is bad. Like, really bad."

"Says who?" Star said.

Dax smacked her forehead, her eyes doubling in size as she stared at Star. "Says who?" she repeated. "Star, have you lost your mind? You know how things work around here. There are rules in place for a reason—"

Star scoffed, while the more timid ones of the group—Echo, Rose, and Asako—watched her curiously.

"Rules?" Star said. "Don't you get it? This is all bullshit. All of it. Do you honestly think you're going to ascend when this is over?"

No one responded.

I thought about stepping in—convincing Star that she was getting out of control—but deep down, I didn't want to. Not after what I'd discovered. As I watched her lips flap and her arms flail in every direction imaginable, my anger only amplified. I thought about Mr. Darwin, and how charming he'd been when he presented me his deal.

This whole place was corrupt, and I wanted no part of it.

Grandma, I thought.

Had they hurt her? Killed her? And what about my mother?

"Where do you think Penelope is now?" Star spewed.

Everyone went quiet.

"And her—" She threw an arm out at me. "Do you seriously think they took her overnight for medical testing? Come on. Wake the fuck up."

Everyone's eyes turned on me, and that's when I realized something—we were all in this together. Mr. Darwin couldn't be trusted. He was an Elite like the person who had ordered my people to be slaughtered. He was no better than any of them, and the last thing I wanted was to make a deal with a man like that.

For all I knew, he'd kill me after he got what he wanted.

I couldn't trust him; I couldn't trust anyone.

Danika stepped toward me. "Is this true?"

I swallowed hard, instantly feeling like I'd betrayed all of them. Would they hate me for it? Would they turn their backs on me? I barely knew them, yet I felt like they were the only friends I'd ever had. And already, I'd let them down.

I parted my lips, prepared to tell them everything, when a loud hissing sound bounced off the walls around us. Where was it coming from? What was going on?

"What is—" Danika tried, but she collapsed into the dining room table before falling onto the floor.

Star's eyes widened at me, but no one had the time to say anything.

I felt sluggish—paralyzed, even. I blinked hard and everything went black.

CHAPTER 25

Silverstasia," came a familiar voice.

I opened my eyes, shivering as countless goose bumps erupted all over my skin. Where was I? The air felt cool and moist. I sat upright, and the bed underneath me squeaked.

"I'm rather disappointed."

The light flickered above, revealing a dark figure every few seconds. The man moved toward me, and as the light swung back to the right, I saw a glimpse of his perfectly coiffed hair—it was dark, and combed over on one side only.

"You had one simple task."

A warm, minty scent filled my nose.

Mr. Darwin.

"I never accepted your deal," I said, matter-of-factly.

He laughed, though it didn't sound genuine. If anything, it sounded like he was holding back an angry outburst.

"I don't understand you, Silver." He paced from side to side, then reached for the flickering bulb and twisted it until the light became constant.

Everything around me was gray and cold. Behind Mr. Darwin was a concrete wall with a metal door, and beside the bed I was sitting on, a small silver toilet that looked as dirty as our urine buckets in Lutum.

"You were promised everything, yet you refuse to accept the gifts we offer."

Was he referring to the lottery again? Why did everyone keep bringing that up?

"I hoped I could prove her wrong, but you've made it impossible."

"What are you talking about?" I asked. More importantly, *who* was he talking about?

I rubbed the back of my head. It felt hot and tender to the touch, like someone had beaten me with a torch. What had happened? I remembered standing in my room with the other women... Right before that loud hissing sound.

Mr. Darwin sighed, pinched his nose, and ran a hand through his slick black hair. "All I've ever wanted was the best for my daughter."

"Stop saying that," I said. "I'm not your daughter."

Frowning, he took a heavy step toward me, a dark shadow looming between us.

"Do you have any idea how hard I worked to get you here?" His voice came out rough and grainy.

"I don't care," I said. "You wasted your time. I don't want anything to do with you, the Elites, or this stupid place."

An indent formed at the center of his forehead. What did he have to be so angry about? I was the one who had been taken against my will.

"Was it *you*?" I asked.

He watched me curiously.

"Did you order the attack?" I said.

He scoffed and readjusted his tie. "Your people did that all on their own."

I stood, prepared to lunge at him, when I felt something cold and heavy holding me back by the ankle. The shackle was connected to a rusty chain that slid under the bed. Although I wasn't sure where the other end was connected, I got the feeling that if I tried to attack Darwin, I wouldn't reach him.

Besides, it wasn't like I had any fighting experience. Even if I managed to grab hold of him, what would I do?

"Did you hurt her?" I said through gritted teeth.

His eyes twinkled. Locking his fingers in front of his belly, he raised his stubbled chin. "I presume you're referring to your grandmother."

I stepped forward, the chain clanging against the concrete floor.

"Your grandmother is safe, as is your mother."

I wanted to believe him—more than anything—but I didn't trust him. What if he was lying to keep me calm?

"You don't believe me," he said.

I breathed out hard through my nose.

"Well, let me prove it." He reached for something in his pocket—a little black gadget that shimmered as he pulled it out—and pressed a button.

On the left wall came an image of my mother and grandmother sitting side by side with ropes around their wrists and ankles. They sat tied to chairs, their backs facing each other. In their mouths were old cloths, or rags to keep them from shouting. My grandmother blinked hard, her grayish-green eyes searching the space around her. Above her right eye was a bloody gash, and across her wrinkled chest, a large bruise.

"What the hell are you doing to them?" I snapped.

I took a step forward, but the chain under me rattled again, keeping me close to the bed.

"I never wanted any of this, Silver, but you've given me no other choice."

He turned away from me, and I kicked forward. The chain yanked, then landed hard on the concrete, filling the entire room with a loud metallic sound.

"Don't hurt them! Don't you fucking hurt them!"

The word felt good coming out of my mouth. I'd never sworn before—Grandma always said it was distasteful—yet somehow, it empowered me.

Mr. Darwin turned his head slightly, a faint smile pulling at the corner of his lips. "You seem to make all the wrong choices when given the opportunity, Silver. Let's see if you make the right decision when someone else's life is at stake."

"What do you want from me?" I shouted. I swallowed hard, feeling like if I didn't, my heart might climb out of my chest. Sweat dripped down my forehead and tickled my cheek as it made its way down my face.

"Let them go!" I shouted.

He pressed another button on the small black gadget and the wall went back to looking like concrete.

"Grandma!" I shouted. "Mom!"

He waved dismissively. "They may be on the other side of this wall, but they can't hear you."

I'd never been one for violence, but this

man made me want to wrap my hands around his throat and never let go. Every bone in my body was crying out for me to hurt him. Why? It wouldn't stop what he was doing. For all I knew, Mr. Darwin wasn't even the one doing this. Maybe it was someone else—someone higher up, like the president.

He rubbed the tips of his fingers together as if trying to rid them of Lutum filth. "When someone asks you for your help, Silver, remember this moment. Remember what's at stake."

He turned around, his broad shoulders barely moving as he walked.

"Wait! No!" I kicked my chain again.

Ignoring me, he reached for the door's handle, turned it, and left.

When Ivy entered the cold, dimly lit room, I jolted upright and shivered. How long had I been sleeping?

"Ivy, oh, thank goodness you're here. I-I don't understand what's happening. Please, tell me you know something. What's going to happen? Where did Mr. Darwin go? Are the others safe?"

She ignored me, then turned around and leaned forward. What was she doing? Reaching for something?

Walking backward, she entered the room dragging a silver cart similar to the one Ruliette had rolled into my temporary room. On it were jars of all colors of the rainbow. I stood up, examining the bright colors. They looked like powder, or maybe jelly, and next to these small glass jars were brushes with wooden handles and smooth black bristles.

A craft kit?

"I hope you're proud of yourself," she said through gritted teeth. "Daddy says I don't get to have my suite anymore." Her menacing eyes shot my way. If resentment were poisonous, I'd have collapsed instantly.

"I was this close—" she mumbled to herself, then slammed something on her cart and huffed. "And now there's talk about shutting down the entire program."

I swung my legs to the edge of the bed. "Program? What program?"

Without a word, she reached for a jar of blue powder and grabbed one of the smaller brushes. "Sit still."

It wasn't like I could go anywhere.

"Where am I?" I asked.

Rolling her eyes, she dipped the brush in her blue powder, twirled it a few times, then pulled it out. The color stuck to the bristles, and she brought it near my face.

"You don't have the right to ask questions," she said. "Not after what you pulled."

She brought the brush even closer and I pulled away. "What's that supposed to mean? What did I do to end up in here? Is this because I stood up to the Defenders? Where are the others?"

She scowled at me, her features twisting so drastically that for a moment, I wondered if maybe I'd hallucinated Ivy... maybe she wasn't here at all, and this was someone else.

Her nostrils flared. "Are you kidding me?" She lowered her voice and breathed to control her anger. "You managed to send everyone into lockdown. That's never happened before."

"Why?" I said. "Because we questioned your ways? Because I defended my friend from one of your abusive Defenders?"

"You're given food, water, shelter," she hissed. "What more could you all want? Hm?" With her free hand, she grabbed my chin and held me in place. "Now, don't move."

My eyelids fluttered as she tickled them with her blue-dipped brush.

"What're you doing?" I mumbled, my mouth squished between her fingers.

"Making you presentable."

"Presentable—"

"Shut up, Silver."

I kept my eyes shut.

"Seven years," she said, her breath smelling like a mixture of egg and coffee, or at least what I remembered coffee smelling like. "All you had to do was keep quiet for seven years, and in return, you'd be given immortality."

"But we wouldn't," I said.

She pulled away as if I'd slapped her across the face. "Excuse me?"

"It's all a lie," I said. "They send us off on a train after."

She scoffed again. I was getting tired of how condescending she was, as if my opinions were equivalent to a spoon of dirt.

"Olympus has a system, Silver. But how dare you call us liars—"

"Are you an Elite?" I asked her.

She let go of my face, smacked the brush on her knee, and stared at me. "I will be."

"But you aren't," I said. "At least not yet. What makes you so sure you'll get the serum? What if you misbehave before then? Do you seriously think they'll want you around *forever*? Even more importantly, have you ever seen any Breeders again after their ascension? Have you seen *Penelope*?"

Her eyes narrowed into slits, and I got the sense she wasn't in the mood to explain everything to a worthless Lutum Breeder like me.

"That's enough," she ordered. "Keep quiet and don't move."

She continued to paint my face for a while.

After a few minutes, she set aside her equipment and inspected her work by grabbing my chin and tilting my head from side to side. "There."

When she stood up, I said, "Where are the others?"

"Your friends?" she asked.

I was surprised she'd referred to them as

my *friends* rather than the other Breeders.

"In the same boat as you," she said.

I searched the floor. "A boat? Are you saying—"

She threw her hands in the air. "Oh, for crying out loud. You lot of uneducated—" But she bit her tongue, grabbed her hips, and said, "It's a saying, Silver. It means you're all in the same position."

"In a room like this?" I asked.

"In prison, yes," she said without a care in the world.

"But you can't do that to Star. What about her baby? Mr. Darwin said—"

She rolled her eyes at the sound of his name. "Mr. Darwin knows nothing about anything, and he certainly isn't in a position of power. He's nothing more than a filthy Lutum man with a lot of money, and here in Olympus, money can only take you far if you're willing to bribe the right people."

Filthy Lutum man... I thought. Mr. Darwin clearly hadn't earned everyone's respect simply by building a large fortune.

"And I don't take orders from him," she said. "Your friends will be released if you cooperate."

"Cooperate?" I asked. "How? What do you need?"

I was willing to do anything. I thought of my mom and my grandmother. Mr. Darwin had said something along the same lines—something about cooperating or doing the right thing.

Without a word, Ivy pushed her cart toward the door.

"Where are you going?" I asked.

She knocked on the door, and it opened from the outside. Before exiting, Ivy reached under her cart and pulled out some sort of fabric. She handed it to me. "Change into those, and for God's sake, Silver, do what the woman says."

Woman? What woman? What was she talking about?

I opened my mouth to ask her for more information, but she shook her head and rushed out of the room, wheeling her cart in front of her.

CHAPTER 27

The walk to the elevators felt somber. Unlike the corridors on the upper level, the walls down here were gray and stained with mold or mildew. It *smelled* wet.

How deep underground had they taken me? *Under* the Pillars?

This place seemed even worse than Lutum. No one was around. I glanced behind me, staring down the empty corridor, when the Defender next to me nudged me with something cold. "Walk faster."

I thought back to Grandma and Mother tied to those chairs, and all I wanted to do was cry. If I didn't listen, would they hurt them? Would they punish *them* for my disobedience?

The Defender prodded me again and I skipped a few steps. Why wasn't Ivy the one escorting me? And what about my friends? Were my actions going to affect them?

When we reached the elevators, I followed

the Defender inside. Although I couldn't see his eyes, I knew he was watching my every movement. Maybe he thought I was a threat—someone capable of putting up a fight.

I bent my knees slightly as the elevator floated upward. It didn't stop. It kept going and going, and I wondered if we would reach the top.

The elevator stopped and I straightened my stance.

When the doors opened, my jaw went slack. Everything in front of me sparkled, including the ceiling tiles. Little golden flakes sat across the pearly white tiles, making me want to get down on my knees to examine them.

I'd always heard of gold, but I'd never seen any with my own eyes.

Unlike the plain tube-shaped lights in the Pillars, the ones in this corridor were designed in the shape of flowers, and every single one was different—unique in one way or another. Some lights were smaller; others, bigger and longer. I imagined someone had designed them by hand at the request of someone with a lot of money.

Along the walls ran two solid strips of shiny metal that looked like it was made of pink gold. I didn't know gold came in different colors. Everywhere I turned my head, something twinkled.

As beautiful as it was, it angered me.

How could someone spend so much money on something as simple as a corridor while thousands of people suffered every day in Lutum?

I took a step into the corridor, but the Defender next to me cleared his throat and pointed at something on the floor. I followed his finger to a basket of daisy white slippers that looked as soft as baby bird feathers.

I bent down and grabbed a pair out of the basket, the plush material feeling soft against my palms.

"Am I supposed to put these on?" I asked him.

The Defender nodded.

I wasn't sure why I was being asked to remove my Olympus shoes and put on slippers, but I did as he'd instructed. Once the Defender nodded again, I knew it was safe to keep moving forward.

I was surprised by how quiet my steps were—even quieter than if I'd been barefooted. Every step felt like I was walking on a luxury mattress.

I kept walking until the Defender's footsteps stopped following me.

I spun around. "Why aren't you coming? Where am I going?"

The Defender pointed straight ahead.

I followed his aim, twirling on my heels again, but I couldn't see anything. This corridor seemed to go on for eternity. How long was it? Would it ever end?

When I turned around again, the Defender was marching his way back to the elevator.

"Hey, wait a minute!" I called to him.

I chased after him, but I wasn't fast enough. He slipped through the open elevator doors, pressed a button, and faced me without a word as the pink gold doors swept closed between us.

Sighing, I kept walking. Not being able to hear my footsteps made me feel funny. Now and then, I wondered if maybe this was all a dream or a hallucination.

Any second now, I would wake up in my room, and Star would be running her mouth about how things aren't fair here in Olympus. As much as her loud voice irritated me at times, I would have given anything to be in the same room as her—to be with my friends.

Then, something caught my eye.

At the end of the corridor were two large pink gold doors that took up the entire back wall. Across their surfaces were abstract designs carved into the metal, creating shadows in all sorts of odd places. I drew in slowly, afraid they might blast open and startle me.

But nothing happened.

I inched a bit closer, waved my hand, then cleared my throat.

Wasn't this where I was supposed to be?

I hesitated knocking. It felt like whatever lay beyond those doors was something big... something that would forever change my life. Maybe if I stood here long enough, the Defender would come back for me.

That's ridiculous, I told myself. *There's no going back.*

Sucking in a deep breath, I knocked on the door.

"Come in," came a pleasant voice.

The doors cracked open on their own but only enough for me to slide my finger through and pull. As I did, natural light came flooding toward me, making me squint and turn my head to the side.

When my eyes adjusted, I blinked hard, taking in the scenery before me. Up ahead was a slender figure standing in front of a translucent wall at the back. Or, was that a giant window? It ran across the entire back wall, all the way up to the ceiling.

I blinked again.

"You must be Silver," the woman said.

Her voice was sweet and calm and made me feel safe. Her silhouette, thin and curvy, moved toward me gracefully.

When I didn't move, she gestured me to come inside. "Please, come in."

The large doors closed behind me as I stepped in, and I stood in awe, admiring the extraordinary room. It was the largest room I'd ever seen—almost the size of the Pillars underground. White marble ran across the floors and up the walls, and from the ceiling hung large lights full of crystals and many bulbs.

Mouth agape, I twirled in circles, taking it all in.

"Rather exquisite, isn't it?" she said.

Exquisite was an understatement.

At the far back stood a kitchen with white, spotless appliances that shimmered under the kitchen light. The counters, shiny black stone, looked as smooth as the floors. Atop it was a large glass jug filled with what appeared to be water infused with fresh lemons.

"Would you like a glass?" she asked me.

Unable to speak, I shook my head.

She extended an open palm in direction of the living room, where plush pink sofas sat in the shape of an L. I'd never seen anything like it before. I'd never even *read* about pink sofas before.

"You're... You're President Kane?" I asked.

She moved toward the kitchen island and flicked her wrist. "The name tends to throw people off." She reached for the jug of lemon water, her fingers adorned with sparkling diamond rings. "My father, President Fitzgerald Kane, got sick and passed away about two years ago. I've since taken his position."

When she turned to face me again, I saw her for the first time. Her face reminded me of something you'd see in a painting. With plush lips, perfectly shaped eyebrows, almond-shaped eyes, and prominent cheekbones, she was stunning.

Her white, skin-tight dress, cinched with a golden belt, clung to her body like a glove. Had it been specifically tailored for her? I'd never seen anything so form-fitting in my life. Her silky ash hair sat neatly in a bun at the base of her skull with two braids caressing the tops of her ears on either side. She was in good shape—better shape than most people in Lutum—with toned arms and a flat belly. Although she wasn't young, she wasn't old, either—maybe in her forties or fifties. I wasn't sure how I knew this because she barely had any wrinkles. Her skin, a creamy beige, looked almost as smooth as mine. Maybe it was her hands that gave it away; a few age spots and wrinkles were visible on the skin around her knuckles, and when she caught me looking, she quickly pulled away from the counter and moved her hands out of sight. She sipped on her water and, without smiling, said, "I love my father, God bless his soul, but I believe the touch of a woman is precisely what Olympus has needed all along."

I kept quiet.

She smiled, though it looked more like she'd tasted something rotten. "I realize Olympus has made quite an awful impression on you." She strolled across to the living room, sat down on one of the sofas, and crossed her legs. "I truly want to make the world a better place, Silver, and I hope you can help me."

What was she talking about? How on Earth could I, Silver Blackwood, help the president of Olympus? This woman had it all—power, control, people willing to do her bidding.

"You must be confused," she forced another half-hearted smile and touched her chest. "I'm terribly sorry it's come to this, Silver. To be honest, you took me by surprise." From her pocket, she extracted a small circular mirror and brought it up to her face. With her pinky, she pulled at the skin beside her eye as if trying to spot new wrinkles. Having likely found nothing, she snapped the mirror shut. "You took us all by surprise that day."

"When I refused to come here," I said plainly.

"Your father certainly did not expect that,"

she responded.

My heart skipped a beat. So, it was true. Mr. Darwin was my father. But the way she spoke about him gave me the sense that he irritated her. Either that, or she was disappointed in how his bringing me here had led to so much chaos.

"Your father has a way with words, Silver. And he certainly has a way with money."

She uncrossed her legs and crossed the other one over. "You deserve honesty, and I'm certain you will appreciate my candidness."

All I wanted was honesty.

Slowly, I sat on the sofa across from her, my palms delicately grazing the soft texture underneath me.

"I have a reputation to uphold, as you well know. Olympus has always been a symbol of hope and opportunity. But ever since you rejected our offer for immortality"—her lips curled as if she were walking by the agriculture division—"well, let's just say the Divisions have begun to question things."

"You mean to question *you*," I corrected.

Her eye twitched, and I wondered if maybe I'd spoken out of line.

"Precisely," she said, forcing another smile. "I'm certain you already know Olympus's survival depends on the cooperation of Lutum. After all, we live off the resources provided by your people."

Then why do you treat us like garbage? I wanted to ask. But I didn't. Instead, I kept my mouth shut. It was best to let her do all the talking.

"There was an unfortunate incident the day we extracted you from Division 9."

"An attack," I said.

She pulled her face back slightly as if insulted that I'd finished her sentence.

"A riot." She rubbed her fingers together as if trying to squash dust. "A riot that led to the unnecessary deaths of many of your people."

I gritted my teeth, holding back a slew of inappropriate words that would have probably made her send me back to my cell.

"And believe me when I say that the riot hurts me more than it hurts you."

I breathed in slowly, trying to hold back my rage. How could she say such a thing? In what universe was she more impacted by the deaths of the people I spent my entire life with?

"You see, we have strong beliefs here in Olympus—blood by our hands leads to misfortune."

"You mean it's bad luck if you kill someone on Olympus soil," I said.

It came out sounding sarcastic, but I got the feeling that was what she'd meant by *misfortune.*

She cast her eyes to the ground and smirked. "Precisely. If we can avoid bloodshed on our land, we will."

On our land. I knew this superstition didn't apply to Lutum—the Elites had killed some of our people before. I'd seen it with my own eyes.

"Is that why you use the train?" I asked.

Her eyes widened. Uncrossing her legs, she leaned back into her rich person sofa and watched me carefully, her bright blue eyes making my stomach sink. "I continue to underestimate you, Silver. How did you find out about the train?"

I didn't want to answer but knew that if I didn't, she'd continue to stare at me. "A note. I found it when I got here."

Her jaw muscles popped out on either side of her defined face. "It would appear someone kept this from me."

By someone, she meant Mr. Darwin. But I kept this information to myself. After all, if he had told President Kane, there was no telling what she might have done. At least Mr. Darwin had *tried* to offer me freedom.

She swatted the air. "It doesn't matter. What matters is restoring balance throughout all of Lutum, and I need your help for that."

"And how can I help?" I asked bitterly.

"I need you to pay a visit to the people of Lutum and convince them that you have never been happier."

"You want me to lie."

She leaned forward, grabbed her lemon water from the glass table between us, and took a slow sip. "I want you to make up for the mistake you made. The people of Lutum have decided to strike in your name, and I will not tolerate that."

I rubbed my forehead. As much as I wanted to refuse to help her, there was no getting out of this. Everyone I cared about risked getting hurt.

"If I do this, will you free my friends and family?"

"*Freedom* is a subjective term, Silver. What I can assure you is that your friends will be granted immunity and kept here in Olympus after they have served their time procreating children. And I will also see to it that you, your mother, and your grandmother become permanent citizens of Olympus."

My first reaction was to scoff in her face. The last thing I wanted was to stay in Olympus. But wasn't this what I had wanted all along? A comfortable life for my family?

I thought of everyone else in Lutum. What about them? What about the children?

As President Kane stared at me, her almond-shaped eyes narrowing menacingly, I knew I wasn't in a position to bargain. I was only one person. I couldn't get Olympus to change their politics.

You can try, I told myself.

"I want the people of Lutum to receive better treatment," I said.

Raising one eyebrow, she grinned slightly and leaned back, holding her drink against her belly and placing an arm on the back of her sofa. "Better treatment? And what would better treatment look like to you?"

"Better food," I said. "More tolerance for the weak and elderly. They shouldn't be forced to work until they die. They should be allowed to stop working."

Was I making a mistake? My heart raced as she stared at me, her intimidating eyes making me want to crawl out of my skin.

"Fine," she finally said. "If you can see to it that the people of Lutum stop revolting, I will honor our deal and make it a priority to make everyone's life more comfortable."

Pushing my cheek with my tongue, I thought the offer over. Was she being genuine? Would she actually make those changes to Lutum? She was the president, after all. She was the one who had the authority to make changes like this.

Likely sensing my doubt, she raised a flat palm. "I give you my word, Silver."

"And when is this happening?" I asked.

"When am I going back to Lutum—"

"Now," she said.

CHAPTER 28

Estrelle glared at me with pure hatred as I walked by, guided by two Defenders. Was it because of what happened in Division 9? Had she lost her position as chancellor? I ignored the thin slits of her eyes and made my way to the chariot outside of the Pillars.

Prototypes stopped what they were doing as we walked, only to be scolded by nearby Defenders and told to get back to work.

When I arrived next to the chariot, one Defender offered his hand. I grabbed it, and he helped me up onto the main platform. I held on to the wooden wall positioned behind the lovely black horses, and next to me stood a man with a thick brown mustache, creamy white skin, and broad shoulders who made me wonder if he spent every evening lifting barrels of water.

"You must be Silver," he said kindly. He

offered me a warm hand and I shook it, all at once feeling weak. "I'm Adryan. Adryan Thompson."

My gaze wandered to the multitude of colorful ribbons fastened on his chest. He wore a blue outfit from head to toe, a color I wasn't accustomed to seeing Elites wear, and near his wrists were golden bracelets similar to those that Mr. Darwin had worn with his suit. Only, Adryan's appeared to be made of metal. His hair, the color of earth and snow, matched his short beard. He was a handsome man—the type of man Grandma would have referred to as a *silver fox.*

"If you've never heard of me, I'm Olympus's Peacemaker." He shot a glance at Estrelle, who huffed loudly, turned around, and disappeared into the Pillars. "You'll have to excuse Estrelle. She's been the leader of Division 9 for decades. And since we aren't hosting a lottery in that division for the next three years, well..."

The cart behind us shook as a dozen Defenders climbed aboard carrying heavy-looking guns.

"Why are *they* coming if you're a *Peacemaker?*" I asked.

Adryan smiled. "A precaution. I had no control over the logistics of this event."

With that, he gently snapped the leather reins in his palms and the horses trotted down the dark cobblestone path.

The hard path eventually turned into dirt, and I sat quietly as we moved farther away from Olympus. Around us were vast fields of yellow grass and sand, and above, the sun worked hard to penetrate a thin sheet of clouds. Along the sides of the path were bright red flowers that stood tall as if begging the sun for its heat.

Were those poppies?

I only knew about poppies because Grandma had once told me they held a special significance—something about commemorating a war. There weren't many books on it, and the few that I found were immediately confiscated or burned by Defenders.

I didn't understand why they were so keen on keeping past politics from us. Maybe they were afraid we'd learn a thing or two about revolutions or fighting.

Adryan didn't speak as we rode through the fields. He observed the horizon straight ahead and kept his chin up, the edges of his mustache fluttering in the wind.

The farther away we rode from Olympus, the cooler it seemed to get outside. The clouds thickened as if trying to warn us to stay away from Lutum. The bit of grass that had decorated the fields around us was no more.

Instead, all that remained was dirt. Even the flowers along the path seemed to wilt the closer we came to Lutum.

The chariot rattled on the bumpy road. Likely sensing my discomfort, Adryan looked down at me and placed a large hand over mine. "It's about two minutes like this. Hold on tight."

It wasn't long before the bumpy ride ended, same as he'd promised. When we returned to a smooth surface, he turned to me. "Do you have your lines?"

He sounded sad about it, and I wasn't sure why.

I uncrumpled the piece of paper in my hands and nodded.

"It's best you recite them word for word," he said.

His suggestion had come across as more of a warning, and I understood it perfectly.

If I didn't do as I was told, the Defenders behind me wouldn't hesitate to make me disappear. President Kane only needed me because she wanted the people of Lutum to stop questioning things and to go back to blindly following orders. If I failed this, what use did she have for me? Deep down, I knew she'd take them by force if this approach didn't work.

I ran a finger over the black ink.

My name is Silver Blackwood. You may have

heard of me through a friend or a family member. I know how fast word spreads across the divisions. I want to clarify that I am beyond happy. Happier than I've ever been. I've received the Ambrosia Serum and have never felt better...

My finger slid across the rest of the lines, and I cringed as I read each word.

Lies. Nothing but lies. How could I deliver this message convincingly? Wouldn't the people of Lutum know I was being insincere? Or, would the Defenders keep me at a distance so that no one could see my features?

As we entered Lutum, my stomach sank.

The tall concrete walls surrounding each division looked the same as the day I left—covered in moss and full of uneven cracks. From a distance, the divisions all looked the same. They were all connected by the giant wall, the only thing separating them being more concrete walls. Each division had a large entrance protected by Defenders, and next to each entrance was a number painted in red. I'd never seen the numbering until now. Were those numbers painted in blood?

Adryan guided the chariot to the first division, where a large 1 was painted on the right side of the concrete opening. He yanked on the reins gently, ordering his two black beauties to stop pulling. Glancing over his shoulder, he sat down next to me. "Do you need a minute?" he asked. "Are you ready?"

"Why are you being so nice to me? Aren't you here to make sure I do my job?"

He smirked, his mustache stretching. "Yes, you could say that. But I'm also the friendly face of Olympus, which is why they sent me. To keep the *peace*."

I didn't recognize him, so I wasn't sure what he was talking about. He'd never come to Division 9 to *keep the peace.*

"Believe it or not, I only want what's best for everyone."

I found that hard to believe. People in Olympus only seemed to look out for themselves.

"I understand this is difficult," he said. "You lying to all of these people. But trust me when I say this is the only way to stop more bloodshed."

I lowered my head and read over my lines again.

"Will she keep her promise?" I asked.

Adryan stiffened his posture. "Who?"

"President Kane," I said.

He chewed on his bottom lip. "I assume she made a deal with you." He paused, thinking it over. "I can't say for sure. I'm sorry. I've never actually met the new president, and it's been two years since she's taken her father's place. All I know is that when she wants something, she gets it. And there's a lot she wants."

That did nothing to reassure me, but what did it matter, anyway? I couldn't take a gamble based on the possibility of her not holding up her end of the deal. I had to hope for the best.

I nodded. "I'm ready."

"You sure?" he asked, staring at me, his eyes soft.

I was beginning to understand why he'd earned the title of Peacemaker. It was as if he'd spent his entire life studying human psychology. I couldn't tell whether he genuinely cared about me, or if he was only practicing psychological tactics on me, but whatever the case, he had a way of making me feel safe.

He stood up, yanked on his reins again, and directed the chariot in through Division 1's entrance. As we strolled inside, Defenders stepped aside, and the ones hiding at the back of our chariot hopped out, guns ready.

A crowd of confused citizens had already gathered near the entrance door. Were they waiting for me? Had it already been announced that I would be coming here? People watched me with a mixture of curiosity and fascination, some stretching their necks to get a good look at me.

Division 1 didn't look all that different from my own—dirt everywhere, slanted wooden houses, and people of all different ages, shapes, and sizes. Everyone wore torn clothing, and as I approached wearing the white and rose robe the president had asked me to wear, I felt awful.

Adryan moved toward the crowd in front of me.

"Hello," he shouted.

No one responded. Instead, they watched him, their eyes looking huge in the middle of their dirt-stained faces. I thought of Rose, and how she'd lost her tongue as a child. Rumor had it that everyone in Division 1 had their tongues cut out. I squinted, trying to see the inside of someone's mouth. Was it true? Was this place *that* cruel?

"I believe there may have been some misunderstanding about this young woman, Silver Blackwood. We have brought her here to speak with you directly. Are you all okay with this?"

People glanced sideways at each other, but no one spoke. When a few nods spread through the crowd, Adryan offered me a hand, encouraging me to step up onto a flat stone next to him.

When I grabbed his hand, he gave me a look that said, *You can do this.*

With trembling legs, I climbed the smooth rock and cleared my throat.

"M-my name is Silver Blackwood." I paused, watching everyone to make sure they were listening. "You may have heard of me through a friend... or a family member." I felt like an idiot. Although I'd memorized my lines, I could tell it sounded like I was reciting them, which I was. I read the lines in my head the way I'd seen them drawn out on the paper. "I know how fast word spreads across the divisions. I want to... I want to clarify that I am beyond happy." *Happy.* This was the most important part of my speech. I grinned as wide as I could, feeling like a fraud. "Happier than I've ever been." My smile grew so wide that I actually started to feel happy. "I've received the Ambrosia Serum and have never felt better. I-I also want you to know that I didn't reject immortality. The truth is, I was taught to look out for others growing up. Since the lottery was a tie, I wanted to give my win to the girl next to me." I paused as features softened throughout the division. "That's the kind of people we are here in Lutum. So please... please get back to work. What you do here saves lives every day—lives of young children in Olympus. If you keep working hard, maybe one day, you'll get to be as lucky as me. I promise you, it's worth it."

A heavy silence spread throughout the division as people nodded, many of them smiling at me.

I felt awful. If only they knew that everything coming out of my mouth was a complete lie. I wanted to shout at the top of my lungs and tell everyone the truth—tell them that Olympus was as corrupt as I'd always believed it to be, and that I hadn't received the Ambrosia Serum; I'd been imprisoned by the Elites and forced to spend the next seven years birthing children, after which I would be sent off on a train to some unknown location and left to rot.

But I couldn't.

I thought of Grandma and her swollen face. If I lashed out now, not only would I condemn these people to death, but I would also be responsible for the death of my grandmother, my mother, and my new friends.

So I bit my tongue and climbed back onto the chariot as hot tears slid down my cheeks.

CHAPTER 29

As we traversed each division, I imagined that my speech would become easier the more I delivered it. It didn't. The more I lied, the more disgusted I became. Division 3 proved more vocal than the first two, with one man shouting, "How do we know they didn't put ya up to this? Like they tore you 'way from yer home when you didn't wanna go?"

As soon as the words came out of this mouth, two Defenders rushed toward him with batons held up in the air.

"There's no need for violence," I shouted, and they backed off as if I were speaking on behalf of President Kane. It was a weird feeling... having the ability to stop Defenders in their tracks. But I knew my false authority was a one-time thing.

"That's a good question," I said, my voice aimed at the confused man. "If I were in your shoes—" I paused, realizing the man wasn't wearing any shoes. "If I were in your position, I'd be asking the same thing."

Adryan took a step toward me, likely afraid of what I might say next.

"I agree that Olympus has a way of making decisions however they see fit," I said.

Adryan tensed.

"But I was born and raised in Lutum. Believe me when I say that my loyalty lies with Lutum."

A knot formed in my stomach. Was I truly about to outright lie to everyone? But then, I thought of something: I wasn't exactly lying. My loyalty still lay with Lutum. The only reason I was standing there to begin with was to avoid more bloodshed. As much as I wanted to tell everyone the truth, I wanted to protect them above all else. And if that meant bending the truth a little bit, then so be it.

The crowd fell silent, and the man who'd spoken first unclenched his fists.

"I may be an Elite now, but I will always put you first," I continued.

If only I were an Elite, I thought. I'd make changes. I wouldn't allow people to suffer the way they did. I reminded myself that if President Kane upheld her part of the deal, their lives could be changed for the better.

My words seemed to calm the man. He nodded and retreated into the crowd of filthy faces.

Adryan gently grabbed my arm and led me back to the chariot. "Well done."

Ashamed, I tried to ignore him. The only comfort I found in all of this was knowing I'd saved that man's life. If I hadn't stepped in, the Defenders would have surely beaten him senseless.

The horse's hooves sounded like gentle thunder as we continued our path. I remained quiet beside Adryan, telling myself that everything would be fine.

"I know this is hard—" he started.

"What would you know about hard?" I snapped back. "You're an Elite... You never age. You have all the delicious food you want. A warm bed. Probably a family. And you must get to travel the lands around here. So don't stand there and act like you know anything about my life."

Pursing his lips, he nodded knowingly. "All right, you got me there. I admit that my life has been easier than yours, Silver, but not as you might think. Like you, I'm a prisoner. I have my orders, and if I don't follow them, I'll receive a one-way ticket out of Olympus."

I stared at him. Was this true? How could he even say that? He didn't look like a prisoner to me.

He sighed. "As I'm sure you've already figured out, I'm one of the Primaries."

He pointed at his crow's feet, though they weren't all that noticeable.

And what was a Primary? I'd never heard that term before.

"I've been around for a long time." He held onto his horses' reins and stared straight ahead as we descended a slanted path.

"President Kane—*Fitzgerald* Kane, who was Alison Kane's father—founded Olympus nearly sixty years ago," he said.

Alison. I assumed he was referring to the new President Kane.

"I know that name," I said. "I read the book on Olympus's origin."

Adryan seemed surprised by this, likely wondering where I might have found such a book. I held back the part about Mr. Darwin allowing me to sleep inside Olympus for one night.

"I was forty-two years old when my father purchased a kit for our family," he said.

I remembered something about kits, too. Apparently, only the wealthy were able to afford the high price.

"Fitzgerald somehow found a way to buy out Dr. Elizabeth Ryskee, the serum's creator."

"Why are you telling me all of this?" I was getting impatient. I didn't care about how Olympus had started out. All I knew was that it was corrupt, and I wanted nothing to do with it.

He sighed. "This wasn't Dr. Ryskee's dream, Silver. She didn't want any of this. The greed, the corruption, the thirst for power. But after we—my family and other families who were wealthy enough to purchase the serum—received our dose, everything changed. Fitzgerald increased his prices, and one thing led to another. As I'm sure you've read, the war started."

"Yeah, I read about that," I admitted.

"Many people who received the serum were slaughtered at the hands of civilians. Some were cut to pieces and stomped on after being accused of playing God... of being abominations. My family swore fealty to Fitzgerald that year; it was the only way to be saved... to be protected from the mobs. We were brought to a private island—or at least those of us who remained—and kept there for nearly three years as the world fell apart. Since fortunes had been spent on purchasing the vials, an unprecedented economic crash followed, and one thing led to another as people turned on each other."

I swallowed hard. I hadn't read about any of that in the book. Why had they excluded this information? History made it sound like envy caused the world to fall apart—like we deserved to be punished for having been so jealous of the Elites. Sure, there may have been envy, but Fitzgerald's greed was mostly responsible for the anger. He'd excluded so many people, basically declaring that unless you were extremely rich, your life was meaningless and you were meant to expire.

"And then President Kane created Olympus," I said matter-of-factly.

Adryan whistled and pulled on his reins, ordering the horses to stop in front of Division 4.

"Exactly," he said. "You may think my life is full of joy, Silver, but like you, I simply do what I'm told."

"Haven't you ever thought of maybe taking a stand?" I asked.

He hushed me with a gentle touch to my shoulder and shook his head. Glancing back toward the chariot full of Defenders, he said, "I have a wife and a daughter, Silver. I can't risk anything happening to them."

"Yeah, well, if everyone keeps thinking that way—"

He smiled and squeezed my shoulder. "Come on. You're getting good at these speeches."

CHAPTER 30

I delivered my speech repeatedly to the remaining divisions. No one spoke up; everyone simply listened, which made me feel worse. It meant they believed everything I was saying. It wasn't until we reached my division—the ninth one—that something happened.

As we drove toward my concrete wall, where a large 9 was painted in bright red, I thought I might vomit. How could I face the survivors? How could I tell them to get back to work when so many of them had given their lives fighting for me? Would I be able to concentrate long enough to remember my words?

But as we approached Division 9's entry path—the one that connected to the main trail—Adryan made a clicking sound with his mouth and ordered his horses to move faster.

"What are you doing?" I asked, twisting my

torso to see my home as we swept by.

"President Kane's orders," he said.

"What orders?" I snapped.

Without thinking, I reached for the reins in his hands, forcing him to pull them back. His horses neighed and kicked wildly, and the chariot swerved off the path.

"Silver!" Adryan hissed, fighting me off.

He managed to regain control of his horses then ordered them to stop. He frowned down at me, likely preparing to give me some big speech about how dangerous it was to reach for someone else's reins, when I crossed my arms over my chest. "Why did she ask you to skip my division? She doesn't think I can handle it?"

His features softened. "Silver, I don't know, I'm sorry. I don't make the rules—I follow them."

"Blindly." I dug my fingernails into my arms to stop myself from saying something worse.

A loud bang came from the chariot wall behind us. "What's going on? Keep moving!" came a husky voice.

Adryan's eyes shot in the direction of our armed passengers. "Please don't make this any more difficult than it has to be."

"I want to see my people."

"I understand, but I have direct orders, and if we stop, there's no telling what the president

288

might do. To me or to you."

I understood why Adryan was afraid, but it didn't make any sense to me. What right did she have to keep me from my people? From Grunwalt? From Kiatha? Or even from the new boy I'd met—Rolie?

My stomach sank. What if they'd been slaughtered along with the rest of them? What if she'd lied to me and everyone was dead? I needed to know.

"Silver," Adryan said sternly. He reached for my shoulder but I pulled away. "We need to keep moving. *Please*."

"Whoa, whoa," shouted a voice in the distance.

Out from my division's entrance came a flat cart pulled by two brown and white horses. What was that thing? The man responsible for driving it whipped a long, leather strap at his horses' rear ends, trying to get them to straighten out. They must have turned too sharply—the cart was caught on one of the concrete walls.

Beside him were two Defenders walking back and forth, trying to figure out how to dislodge the cart.

"Back up!" one Defender shouted, waving backward.

They went at it for a minute or so until whatever was caught dislodged, and out came the cart, carrying a large load that I couldn't quite make out. Most of it looked like hay and blankets, which didn't make any sense—we didn't have hay in our division, and they were leaving, not entering.

What also struck me as odd was the cart's construction. Its walls were low, and it was much larger than the typical carts that were sent to our division every morning for resource pickup.

If they weren't bringing fruits and vegetables out, what was in there?

"It's time to go," Adryan said.

He became impatient and reached for his horse's reins.

I squinted, trying to get a better look at the cart, when out from underneath a beige blanket came a white, limp hand.

I blinked hard, feeling like my heart might give out.

Bodies. Dead bodies piled atop one another.

Adryan gave his horses the order to start moving, and although I knew the safest thing to do was sit quietly next to him, I couldn't do it. Something inside me told me to jump off... to find out what exactly the Elites were up to.

I jumped out of the chariot, Adryan shouting behind me, and ran toward the cart.

"Hey!" shouted a Defender. "Get her out of

here!"

"What is this?" I shouted. "How many bodies are in there? How many people did you kill?"

He stomped toward me, but I hurried past him and ran straight into my division, knowing full well that any second now, I might get shot in the back. But I didn't care. I needed to see it for myself.

The moment I entered, I thought I might throw up. My knees buckled and I stumbled sideways, nearly falling over.

This couldn't be.

"Silver!" came Adryan's voice behind me.

What I saw before me was a division I didn't recognize. Where there had once been hundreds of citizens working in the gardens, only a few dozen remained. Next to the garden beds, homes had been burned to the ground, leaving behind nothing but debris, charred wood, and piles of ashes.

My home, too, was gone.

"Silver!" Adryan tried again.

Rapid footsteps rushed toward me, and all I could think to do was run. I ran to the remains of my home and started yanking on beams of wood. "Grunwalt! Kiatha!"

"It's no use," came a soft voice.

I turned sideways to find a Rolie I didn't recognize. When I had first met him, he'd been so handsome with that crooked smile and playful tilt of the head. But now, his scraggly chestnut hair was covered in dirt and blood, and one of his eyes was as red as a cherry.

"They killed them before they burned the place down," he said, his voice raw.

I wiped my face with my forearm. "But... how? Why? Why did this happen?"

He shrugged with one shoulder. "Because we're nothing more than property, Silver. They didn't like us asking questions or making demands that you be returned."

I slapped a hand over my mouth, as the bile rose. It was all my fault.

"This isn't your fault," he said as if reading my mind. "The Elites did this. Not you."

"Silver!" Adryan's voice drew nearer. Behind him came heavy footsteps and a bunch of Defenders carrying guns. Adryan immediately turned around to face them, raised two hands, and said, "I'll take care of this."

The Defenders lowered their guns but didn't back off.

"Silver, my dear," Adryan said, his voice almost a whisper.

He moved toward me carefully, as if trying to approach a wild animal.

"Whatever they're promising you, Silver, don't you believe it," Rolie said. "You hear me?"

"Promising?" I repeated. "How do you know

292

they're promising—"

"We have to go," Adryan said.

Rolie shot him a nasty glare. "Because you wouldn't be out here unless they needed you for something."

He was right.

"If President Kane finds out I was here—" Adryan started.

"President Kane?" Rolie growled. He closed his eyes and exhaled slowly. "You're working with the president?"

"I don't have a choice!" I shouted. "She has my grandmother and my mother!"

Rolie scoffed, making me feel like a child. "And you believed her?"

I breathed out hard, not wanting to explain the whole story. Alison Kane hadn't been the one to tell me about my grandmother—Mr. Darwin, my supposed father, *showed* me my grandmother through the wall. How was I supposed to explain all of that?

"I saw her," I said, matter-of-factly.

Again, a scoff. "Don't be stupid, Silver. They can grant immortality. You don't think they can create false images? Your grandmother—"

Adryan grabbed me firmly by the arm. "We need to go. Now."

Behind him, a handful of Defenders moved in on us with guns aimed at our chests.

Adryan yanked on me, trying to pry me

away from Rolie. I shoved him hard and kicked him in the shin.

He sighed through wide nostrils as if to say, *I'm sorry it's come to this.* He lunged for me, wrapped me in his strong arms, and jabbed something into my neck.

"I'm sorry, Silver," he said. "I truly am. But this is for your own good."

I blinked once, twice, before his features swirled and distorted.

Rolie raised a solid fist and charged for Adryan, smashing him in the jaw. "Let her go! Let her go!"

Countless footsteps splattered in the mud around us as dark figures got involved.

Rolie let out a pained grunt, and then another, and another.

I watched as a blurry version of him fell to the ground, surrounded by a handful of Defenders beating on him. He became smaller and smaller as Adryan pulled me away.

"They—they killed her, Silver!" Rolie shouted. "Y-your grandmother. And your mother! They were the first to be slaughtered!"

Another loud grunt, a crushing sound, then silence.

I tried to scream out and tell them to stop, but I couldn't. Everything went black, and I drifted away.

CHAPTER 31

I licked my parched lips as a bunch of loud voices filled the air around me.

It sounded like they were arguing about something. I wanted to sit up and see what was going on, but I couldn't. I was tied down on my back. The only thing I could do was turn my head sideways, and even that required a lot of strength.

Why was I so exhausted? I managed to crack one eye open.

There were three men in total, and they spoke with animated gestures.

"You can't do this," came a pleading voice.

I recognized it. Adryan?

Footsteps paced from one end of the room to the other. I watched as the three men moved around like shadows, their features barely visible. The only light entering the room seemed to come from the open door behind them.

I inhaled, filling my nose with the same musty smell from earlier.

Was I back in the basement? In that room made of concrete?

"There has to be another way," Adryan said.

"What choice do I have?" growled one of the other men. "They're *her* orders." He moved in on Adryan, their faces almost touching. "What did you think was going to happen? You should have had better control over her."

This man was taller than the other two. He spoke with a rounded back and tight fists like he was prepared to get physical if necessary.

Then, Mr. Darwin spoke. "This isn't the girl's fault. Please, have President Kane reconsider—"

He stepped forward, his glossy black hair coming into view. He wore the same suit he'd had on earlier, and for the first time, he didn't look calm or composed. He looked like he was panicking. When a strand of hair fell out of place, he ran a hand over it, securing it at the top of his head.

"President Kane already gave her orders," said the tall man. "Now, unless you want to end up like the people in Division 9, I suggest you get out of the way."

"No, please—" Mr. Darwin said.

Then, Adryan said, "This is all a misunderstanding. Give the girl another chance."

The sound of weapons being drawn came from the distance, and more shadows appeared.

"Please!" Mr. Darwin cried out.

But it was no use. Both he and Adryan stood helplessly, surrounded by armed Defenders.

Mr. Darwin shoved his way past them and rushed toward me. He knelt on one knee, smiling. At least, it looked like he was smiling. I could barely see anything. What I did feel from him, however, was sadness.

I flinched when his warm finger grazed my cheek.

"I'm sorry, my sweet Silver. I'm so sorry. I hoped this would end differently."

End differently?

In that moment, everything came back to me—Grandma, Mother, my friends, President Kane, Lutum. Oh, no, what had I done? How could I have been so stupid?

He leaned forward, kissed my forehead, and said, "I did everything I could."

Standing, he disappeared into the darkness.

I tried to sit upright again, but both my wrists and ankles were fastened tightly.

I wanted to scream—to demand that I be told what was going on—but I didn't have the strength. I couldn't even open my other eye.

Instead, I drifted in and out of consciousness as two Defenders removed my restraints and took me somewhere else.

I woke up to a steady, hypnotizing sound—a sound I'd heard once before.

A train?

This time around, I managed to open both eyes. I sat inside a train again—the exact same train that had brought me here. All around me was cherry-colored wood and red seats with metal frames. Golden borders enveloped the dirty windows, and from the dome-shaped ceiling hung small lights similar to those in President Kane's room—lights full of crystals and a multitude of bulbs. But they weren't anything close to the ones in the president's room. They weren't as large or as nice and looked to be several hundred years old.

I gripped one of the nearby metal posts and forced myself to sit upright. As I inhaled, a strong perfume entered my nose. I recognized that smell; I'd smelled it when I first arrived here.

Then came the smell of a citrus cleanser, which told me someone had recently been here to tidy up. Had they been expecting me? I pulled myself up even higher onto one of the seats, but I tumbled back down onto my knees when the train shook gently, making a clickety-clacking noise.

I tried again, this time rising to my unsteady feet. I caught myself against one of the metal support poles, then slowly lowered myself into the nearest seat. Next to it was a large dusty window with four long strokes running through the filth. Finger marks?

With my elbow, I scraped at the dust until a clear circle formed at the center of the window. Outside were hills, mountains, and landscapes unlike anything I'd ever seen before. Everything was green—not yellow, or brown.

The scene swept by so fast that I blinked several times and even looked away to avoid getting dizzy. If I stared long enough, the nearby landscape blended into a neutral-colored blur, but in the distance, the scenery moved at a slower pace. So I focused on staring farther ahead.

"Mountains," I breathed, resting my face against the window.

I wanted to reach out and touch the tips of the mountains to see if they were as cold to the touch as I'd read about. From this distance, they looked minuscule as if not even real at all. I'd always heard that mountains were enormous.

How far away were they to look so small?

For a moment, I forgot where I was and smiled as I admired the beauty in front of me.

As the train continued to follow the railway, the mountains barely moved. They simply sat there, calm and collected, as if nothing in the world mattered. If only I were that calm, I thought, pressing a firm hand over my beating heart.

Grandma used to tell me that a person's greatest weapon was the ability to remain calm in a stressful situation. *Grandma...* I suddenly remembered. Rolie. Mother.

Was it true? Were they really gone? My throat swelled so much that a throbbing ache spread down my neck. It couldn't be. I thought of Grandma's sweet, wrinkled face and didn't know whether to burst out crying, to scream, or to stand up and start breaking anything I could grab.

So instead, I sat still, gazing at the mountains beyond the horizon as reality slipped from my grasp. Maybe if I sat here long enough, I would wake up somewhere else—in Olympus, maybe, next to Grandma.

I rested my cheek against the cool glass, wanting to feel anything but this pain. Still, I couldn't hold it back. My lips trembled, and hot tears streamed down my face.

Hold it together.

300

But I couldn't.

Instead, I sobbed uncontrollably until my lips slobbered and I could barely breathe.

I pictured Grandma's face again and reached into the air, wanting to graze her skin. What I wanted most of all was to touch her again, one last time... even if only to say goodbye.

How could she be gone forever? I had seen her. Mr. Darwin had shown me both my mother and grandmother in the room next to me. Had it all been a trick? A tactic to get me to cooperate? Had he done it to manipulate me, or to try to save me from President Kane's wrath?

I didn't know what to believe.

So I stopped thinking.

Instead, I leaned against the window and cried until I could no longer cry.

Hours passed as the train continued its journey, filling my gut with anxiety. I'd never traveled this far away before. The most I'd ever traveled was the distance between Lutum and Olympus, which had only been a few days ago.

The sun began to set, filling the sky with colors similar to the rainbow. It was heavenly, and I wondered if Grandma was now sitting on one of those clouds, watching my little train move through hills and mountains.

Would she protect me? Was she still even

here? I'd never known what to believe when it came to the afterlife. Although I'd read books on various religions, the discussion of it was never tolerated in Lutum. Now, I understood why. President Kane, along with her Elites, wanted the people of Lutum to revere them, not invisible beings.

I closed my eyes, imagining what it might feel like to die.

Wasn't that what was about to happen, anyway?

Weren't they taking me somewhere far away from Olympus to slaughter me?

Maybe that was for the best. Maybe this life wasn't worth living, especially now that Grandma was gone. Would she be waiting for me?

Although I wasn't certain that I was being taken away to be killed, I knew how awful Olympus was, and I also knew that President Kane was capable of anything.

You can't let them win, I told myself. *Maybe there's still a chance to make things right.*

Grinding my teeth, I envisioned myself fighting against my opponent, whoever that may be. When the time came, I'd put up a fight. I wasn't yet sure how, but I'd give it my all to take them down.

A door creaked open behind me and footsteps approached.

I was out of time.

CHAPTER 32

S ilver?"

I recognized that voice.

I twirled around in my seat to find Danika standing near the door, her greasy, matted hair hanging loose over one shoulder. She stared at me, her eyes doubling to the size of chicken eggs.

"Silver!" She rushed over to me.

I blinked hard. "Danika! What—what's going on?"

I was excited to see a familiar face—to know I wasn't alone on this mysterious train.

"What are you doing here?" she asked.

She ran to me and threw her arms around my neck. "I thought... I don't know what I thought."

When she pulled back, I said, "What are you doing here? Is this because of me?"

She scrunched her nose as if I'd lost my mind. "What're you talking about? How would this be because of you?"

I wanted to tell her everything—Mr. Darwin, my chat with President Kane, my visit to Lutum, but there were so many emotions boiling inside me that I couldn't bring myself to say a word. I felt guilty for having ever even considered Mr. Darwin's offer. Maybe if I'd rejected him right away, none of this would have happened. Or, maybe if I'd tried harder...

No, it didn't matter.

The truth was, Danika, along with all of my other friends, would have ended up right here on this train at one point or another. The only difference is they would have spent years giving birth to children they would never have the pleasure of holding or loving.

"Come on," Danika said, tugging gently on my torn sleeve.

"Where?" I asked.

When I didn't budge, she said, "To see the others," like it was obvious.

Others?

I followed her through the train, a set of doors, and then through another series of spaces that looked identical to the one I'd woken up in. How many of these train *rooms* were there?

"Two more," she said, smiling over her shoulder.

I admired Danika for how cheerful she

always seemed to be, even in a situation like this. It was like nothing fazed her, and no matter how bad things got, there was always hope.

When we stepped through the last door, I couldn't believe what I was seeing.

Star.

Dax.

Rose.

Echo.

Asako.

Everyone was here.

Echo stood first, gripping the back of a seat for support. She smiled sweetly at me. "Silver. We thought they took you."

I shook my head. "I'm okay. A lot happened."

Dax swung her body out of her seat, smacked a solid hand on my shoulder, and said, "Good to have you back."

Why was everyone being so nice to me? The guilt was eating me up inside. If only they knew about the deal I'd been offered, or that I was already familiar with the train and Olympus's empty promises.

Asako sat quietly close to Star, watching me. I never knew what she was thinking and it made me uneasy. Did she know the truth? Her gaze felt accusatory, but it probably wasn't. Asako was just reserved.

"I-I'm sorry," I said to everyone.

Dax pulled her face back. "Sorry? You didn't do this, Silver."

"Kind of," I said.

No one spoke. Not even Star, who sat at the farthest corner of the room, looking about as awful as I felt, if not worse. What was going on with her? She didn't move or make eye contact, and instead, stared absentmindedly at the wooden walls across from her.

Dax gave me a stern look. "This isn't your fault, okay?"

I wanted to thank her for her words, but my gaze lingered on Star. She seemed even worse than before. Had something happened? Had they done something to her?

"What's wrong with her?" I asked.

No one responded and the air became heavy.

Something had happened.

I wanted to sit next to her, but Dax stuck out an arm, blocking me from getting any closer. "She needs time."

"Time?" I said.

I made myself taller by standing on the tips of my toes, and then I saw it. Her round belly was gone. She sat with her back against the wall and trembling arms folded over her blood-stained shirt.

"They cut her baby out," Danika said.

My heart pounded so hard I thought I might

collapse. Slowly, I lowered myself into the nearest seat. "What? Why? How could—"

But I stopped talking. No matter how many questions I asked, no one would have the answer I wanted.

There was only one answer: Elites were cruel and heartless.

But then, another question entered my mind. If the Elites couldn't populate among themselves, how could they get rid of their Breeders? Didn't they *need* us?

I recalled Star getting mouthy, and how she thought she was immune from being thrown out of Olympus. I had believed her. So, why were we here? Were they planning on hosting another lottery for several winners? Was that President Kane's big plan? Maybe the only way to bring about peace after what had happened was to offer the people of Lutum something exciting, like a special once-in-a-lifetime lottery.

"I thought they needed us," I said.

Danika sighed. "So did we. But Rose overheard something."

Rose lowered her head and pulled her hair over her creamy brown shoulder. Then, she locked eyes with Danika and started making hand gestures.

Sign language? I wished I understood, but I couldn't make out what she was saying.

Danika watched her, nodding. "Something about a doctor. Dr. Barek, or something."

Dr. Bartek, she meant. He was the man I'd seen exiting a strange room the night Mr. Darwin made me the deal. What could he possibly have to do with any of this? He seemed kind.

Rose continued making hand gestures.

"She overheard two people talking. They mentioned Dr. Barek and how he finished his project."

I considered correcting her pronunciation of his name, but I wasn't yet ready to admit everything.

"Project?" I asked. "What project?"

"That's what we're trying to figure out," Danika said.

Rose made a few final motions and Danika added, "President Kane's the one who gave the order to get rid of us."

I clenched my fists. She'd seemed so genuine—wanting nothing but the best for Olympus and Lutum. How could I have been so stupid? I should have shouted to all of Lutum as loud as I could... warned them of Olympus's corruption. It may have started a war, yes, but the people of Lutum deserved the truth; they deserved a chance to fight back.

Now, because of me and my lies, they'd return to being treated like garbage... to serving Olympus and praying and hoping for an annual opportunity that was also nothing more than a lie.

It didn't make any sense. More than anything, I wanted to know what President Kane had planned. Was she going to punish the people of Lutum? Would things get worse, or would she find a way to make everyone happy?

Dr. Bartek's project, I thought.

I closed my eyes, returning to the day I'd met him. He had come walking out of some room, his back to me. When he had spotted me behind him, he'd jumped as if I'd caught him doing something wrong. Why had he been so on edge? What was he trying to hide?

Come on, Silver, think.

And then, the memory returned.

Cylinder tubes. Skin-colored textures. Grimy fluids.

That was it.

"I have more information," I said.

Echo rested a slender arm on the back of her seat. "What do you mean? What information?"

"I met that doctor. His name is Dr. Bartek. There's a lot I haven't told you. But I saw something. When he stepped out of this strange room... I looked inside. There were weird tubes filled with fluids, and inside, things that looked to be made of human skin."

Everyone but Echo crinkled their noses. "Incubators," she breathed, her thick bottom lip hanging loose.

"What's an incubatator?" Danika asked.

I'd never heard the term, either.

"Incubator," Echo corrected. "Artificial wombs." She jumped up and sat on her knees, looking more alert than I'd ever seen her before. She tapped her lips and searched the ceiling as though fishing for old information in her brain. "It's a plausible concept. I mean, think about it—if the Elites can manage to sustain their own reproduction laboratory, why bother with us Breeders at all? We require food, shelter, and constant monitoring. If they're capable of growing babies—"

Dax laughed out loud. "Growing babies. Do you hear yourself, Echo? Where did you hear something like that? Out of a science fiction novel?"

Echo looked insulted. "Science books," she said like it was obvious.

I could tell by the way Echo spoke that she did a lot of reading—maybe even more than me.

Echo's focus shifted on me. "How did you see Dr. Bartek? Is there anything else you can tell us?"

I sighed. There was no escaping the truth. "In Olympus," I admitted. "When I met my

312

father."

Everyone's eyes bulged, and in the background, a fuzzy version of Star watched me.

"It's a bit of a long story, but I'll tell you everything," I said. "You might want to sit down."

CHAPTER 33

I clenched my teeth, waiting for everyone to accuse me of being a traitor.

But they didn't.

Instead, Danika listened to my every word, her chin resting on her knuckles. "Your dad, huh?"

"Why aren't any of you reacting to the fact that I almost took a deal behind your backs?" I said.

Dax stared blankly at me. "Why would we be angry about that? No offense, but if I'd been offered a deal like that, I would have probably taken it in a heartbeat."

I searched Danika who shrugged awkwardly. "Um, yeah. Me too. What choice did you have, Silver? In the end, we were all ending up on this train. I mean, it's extremely admirable that you didn't take the deal. If you had, you'd be sleeping in a comfortable bed right now. Not sitting in this train, wondering where we're heading."

I felt better.

I wanted to thank them for understanding—for being more supportive than I felt I deserved—but there was a more pressing matter at hand: Dr. Bartek's project.

"I would rather die before accepting any deal from those animals," came Asako's voice.

With jaw muscles popping, she glared out through the train's dusty window.

"So, you think you saw incubators," Echo said, ignoring Asako's remark.

She then swiped the air with her finger as if reading through pages of an invisible book.

I nodded, but she didn't see me. "I mean, I don't know anything about incubators, but the skin inside looked like human skin." When Echo still didn't look at me, I turned to the others. "What's she doing?"

Danika smirked. "Reading."

"Photographic memory," Echo said, now squinting.

I wanted to ask her how it was that she'd read so much as a child. Where did she get her books in Lutum? I was happy to know that books circulated in other divisions.

Then, she tapped the air abruptly with her index finger. "That's right. The concept was being revolutionized several decades ago. Both artificial wombs and embryos."

"Artificial embryos." Danika laughed. "That's not possible."

"Neither is immortality," Asako said matter-of-factly.

Was she being sarcastic? She didn't smile, nor did her features soften. Instead, she continued to observe the distant mountains as I'd done a bit earlier.

"So let's say this is true," I said. "That means they don't need us anymore. Will they stop doing the lotteries?"

Dax plopped herself down again, her legs slightly parted. "I doubt it. Think about it. The lottery is what encourages people to work hard. They aren't going to tell anyone what they've done. They'll probably keep the lottery going and dispose of the winners."

An eerie silence filled the cabin as the train rattled.

"She's right," Danika said.

"So, what do we do now?" I asked.

Asako huffed, clearly annoyed by our conversation. "What do we *do*? There's nothing we *can* do. Don't you get it? We're all going to die."

"Asako, we get that you've been through a lot," Dax said. "But we don't need this negative—"

"A lot?" Asako sneered. She slowly made her way toward us, her posture hunched. "This isn't about Olympus, or about what we've been through. Open your eyes. Wake up. We're on the train. Don't you get it? There's nothing after this."

"That's not true," Star said, her voice hoarse. "Penelope—"

"Penelope left a note before she even knew where she was going!" Asako shouted.

Her voice sounded strained, like she'd never shouted before.

"Penelope is dead," Asako said. "The sooner you all accept that, the sooner—"

The door next to Star swung open, and in came two Defenders.

Everyone stiffened.

Their shielded faces scanned the space around us before they bent forward and grabbed Star by the arm.

"Let her go!" I charged at them.

One of the Defenders kicked me in the stomach, bringing me to my knees.

Star tried to pull away, causing fresh blood to spill from the cut on her belly. "Let me go, you pieces of shit!"

But it was no use. The Defenders gripped her around the belly and throat and dragged her out through the door. Dax rushed by me and tried to turn the handle.

"It's locked!"

Danika did the same, shaking the handle so

wildly it sounded like it might snap off. When the door still didn't open, she smashed her fists against it. "Let her go!"

I held onto my aching stomach as drool slid down my chin. I'd never been kicked in the stomach like that before. Would I ever breathe normally again?

"You okay?" Echo asked.

I didn't feel okay, but I couldn't give up now. Slowly, I stood up.

Rose started making wild hand gestures again and Danika said, "I don't know. None of us do."

"They're probably killing us off one by one," Asako said impassively.

Dax raised a fist at her, but Danika stepped between the two of them, her red hair sweeping behind her back. "Stop it. Both of you. This isn't the time to turn on each other."

"Danika's right," Echo said. "Statistically speaking, we outnumber them."

"No one gives a shit about statistics," Dax growled. She ran her hands through her dark, curly hair. "We need a strategy."

Echo scratched her chin. "Well, yeah, and statistics play a part in that."

Dax sighed. "All right, so what do you propose?"

Still scratching her chin, Echo inspected the floor, the walls, the window. "You aren't going to like my idea."

Asako planted two hands on her hips. "As long as it doesn't involve jumping off this train—"

Echo bit her bottom lip. "Um, kind of."

Dax threw her arms in the air. "You have got to be kidding me."

CHAPTER 34

W ait," I said, grabbing Echo's arm. "We can't."

Echo looked at me as if I were trying to make her repeat the word *Hippopotomonstrosesquippedaliophobia*. It had always stuck with me, making me giggle being that it meant the fear of long words.

"We can't take off and leave Star behind," I said.

It was obvious that Star's abduction was weighing on everyone.

"I understand," Echo said. "But she's probably already dead and the longer we wait to run, the higher our odds are of meeting the same fate."

It took me a few seconds to absorb her words. I didn't understand how she was being so cold and matter-of-fact about it.

Star is probably already dead?

"Okay, and what if she isn't?" I said.

"Shouldn't we at least try to help her?"

Danika tugged at her fingers nervously then glanced sideways at Dax. I didn't blame them for wanting to run. In Lutum, we were raised to look out for ourselves. It was how we survived. If the Defenders decided to bash on someone, everyone else knew to shut their mouths and mind their business if they didn't want the same beating, or worse.

We were programmed to save our own skin.

"You guys go ahead. I need to try to do something," I said.

"Silver!" Dax said. "Be realistic, here. We have the chance to run. If you try to go after Star, you risk your own life. You risk all of our lives."

I didn't care. I had to try something.

I searched the cabin, hoping to find a weapon I could use. Yes, I was way in over my head, but if I left now, knowing I hadn't even tried to help my new friend, I'd never forgive myself. It wasn't right.

"What are you looking for?" Danika asked, searching the cabin with me.

"A weapon. Something."

Asako sighed. "Is this necessary? What chance do we have against armed Defenders?"

I snapped my head up. "Maybe if more people stopped thinking that way, we wouldn't live in a world like this. Everyone's scared to stand up. It's ridiculous. We outnumber them. There's no reason for us to be scared."

"We might outnumber them," Danika said softly, no doubt trying to calm me down, "but they're bigger than us and they have weapons."

I knelt and searched under the seats.

"Maybe there's another way," she added.

"We're wasting time," Asako said.

Suddenly, the back door opened up again, and in came the two Defenders from earlier. We all froze, and Echo stiffened as the guards moved in on her. They grabbed her by the arm and started pulling, and I did the only thing I could think of.

I shouted as loud as I could and charged straight for them again.

Behind me, Dax did the same, and then Danika and even Rose.

I tumbled against the first Defender, feeling like I'd run into a concrete wall. Not only was he large and robust, but his uniform was made of some thick compact material. It felt hard and inflexible against my fists.

"Let her go!" I shouted, shoving him as hard as I could.

The first Defender tumbled backward, catching himself on the second Defender.

"We've got ourselves a hero," he growled as he stumbled.

Dax shoved her way past me and swung a fist at the second Defender's face shield. It cracked in half, spiderwebbing from top to bottom, but remained intact.

Keep fighting. We can do this.

Somehow, I managed to pull Echo out of their gloved hands. As they stumbled to regain their footing, I charged again, this time, aiming my shoulder at the first Defender's torso.

But the moment I tackled him in the stomach, I knew I'd made a mistake. He used my momentum against me, pulling me through the door behind him. We tripped into the other room together.

"Silver!" someone called out.

Right before the door closed, I caught a glimpse of the second Defender extracting what appeared to be some sort of electric metal rod—a spiked black stick with fiery blue spitting wildly at one end.

"No!" I shouted.

The first Defender elbowed me in the face, nearly dislocating my jaw. As my head rocked back and my surroundings blurred, he dragged me through several series of doors. As I slid through the narrow aisles, I tried to grab the legs of nearby seats, but it was no use—I was too weak and disoriented.

I couldn't stop what was happening.

"Since you want to be a hero," he growled,

"you can go next."

Go next? Where was I going? What did that even mean?

"Rocky terrain, too," he said. I could hear the smile on his face. "Should be a nice landing."

Landing?

A powerful gust of wind blasted into the space around me, sending my hair into a chaotic frenzy. I squinted out of an open side door as dark scenery flashed by us. Grass, trees, hills—we were moving so fast that it all blended as one.

The man grabbed me by the back of my neck, paralyzing me. I wanted to try to hit him, but the pain radiating down my back hurt too much for me to think about anything else.

"Enjoy the ride," he said. "And don't even bother trying to look for your friends. You'll be miles apart."

And with that, he threw me out of the train.

CHAPTER 35

My skull cracked against something hard and sharp, and warm blood trickled down my face.

But that didn't matter.

As much as it hurt, I didn't even have the time to focus on it. I flipped and flopped and tumbled down a steep hill, rolling faster than I ever thought possible. Searing pain exploded in my shoulder as it popped out of its socket.

The rolling went on for what felt like minutes until I slowed, before crashing hard against the base of a tree, my ribs cracking.

Blinking, I gazed up into the night sky at the countless stars.

They didn't look any different from the ones above Lutum.

Were they the same stars? I'd never traveled anywhere before. I wasn't sure if the sky's beauty changed depending on one's location.

Not that it mattered.

I sucked in a quivering breath, feeling like my abdomen might implode.

Everything hurt.

I wanted to get up, but I was afraid that if I did, my ribs would come apart and my arm would dangle at my side, disconnected from my body. So instead, I lay in the dirt as a cool breeze tickled the tip of my nose. It was a welcome distraction from the pain, but it didn't last long.

My eyelids fluttered and everything went dark.

"The trick is to use a fork," Grandma said, poking her wooden fork into the crumbly potato. "See? It's ready."

She pulled the pot of potato and leek soup off the fire and set it aside on our wooden counter. It filled the entire home with a warm, mouthwatering scent that made me want to curl up by the fire and breathe it in for hours.

Near the hearth, Grunwalt and Kiatha laughed as they shared jokes. I always admired their sense of humor. No matter how grueling their days, they always managed to find the energy to exchange old jokes they'd learned over the years.

Listening to them warmed my heart.

Laughter wasn't common in Lutum. People returned to their homes after a long day of work in the garden beds, and more often than not, the village remained silent until the next morning. Grunwalt and Kiatha, however, filled our home with a joy that made me look forward to my evenings.

Well, until Mother showed up.

She walked into the main living space with her head bowed and her dark eyes inspecting everyone. We froze, waiting for some nasty comment to come flying out of her mouth. Surprisingly, today wasn't one of those days. Instead, she shoved Grandma aside, stuck the ladle in the steaming liquid, and scooped out a spoonful of Grandma's creamy recipe.

She didn't thank Grandma for her hard work—not that she ever did. Instead, Grandma smirked and nudged me softly in the ribs— something she did every time she noticed Mother's negative energy weighing down on me. It was like she tried to distract me from it.

Mother eventually left to sulk in her room and I followed Grandma to the hearth with a hot bowl of soup in my palms.

"It's hard when it's someone you love," she said, watching me carefully.

I shrugged and sipped soup off my spoon. It was hard for me to admit that I loved Mother, especially with the way she treated me. It didn't make sense that I would love someone who hated me. But I did. All I wanted was for her to be proud of me—to love me back.

"One day, you'll realize that your mom's behavior isn't a reflection of you," Grandma said.

I found that hard to believe, but I held onto her words.

"You're strong, courageous, and you have a mind of your own." She tapped my forehead with her warm finger and I couldn't help but smile. "You'll do great things, Silver. Don't you ever let your mother get in the way of that."

Grunwalt and Kiatha didn't say anything. They both cleared their throats and moved into the kitchen to snatch some of Grandma's soup. Although they never got involved with feuds between Mother and me, I knew they agreed with everything Grandma said.

No one ever took Mother's side.

"You think I'll do great things?" I asked.

Grandma pinched my nose. "I know it. I can feel it. You're going to make a difference in this world, Silver. All you have to do is follow your heart."

I wasn't entirely sure what she meant by that. We lived in Lutum, after all. What difference could I possibly make? I smiled at her and slurped up the rest of my soup, imagining a world entirely different from Lutum.

I opened my eyes to see the millions of stars sparkling overhead. If it weren't for the excruciating pain in my ribs, I would have found comfort in the view.

"I-I'm sorry, Grandma," I breathed.

Was she watching me? Was Mother with her? Was she ashamed of me? I'd been given a chance to make a difference, and I'd thrown it away. What had I done? Maybe if I'd accepted Mr. Darwin's deal, I could have grown inside of Olympus; I could have made a name for myself and begun taking part in Olympus's political system.

I'd thrown away my only chance.

My throat swelled painfully as I imagined Grandma floating above, smiling down at me. She always showed me love, even when I felt I didn't deserve it. I wanted to cry and scream. How could they have taken her from me? Grandma hadn't done anything wrong. She was innocent. I imagined how terrified she must have been when they came storming into our home, setting the walls on fire.

Had they killed her before the fire—as Rolie claimed—or had they forced her to burn up in the flames?

Thinking about it made me sick to my stomach, so I stared up at the stars instead. It was no use torturing myself. I couldn't change what had happened, and I certainly couldn't help Grandma.

Not anymore.

"I'm sorry," I mumbled, my lips bruised and swollen.

I licked the crusty blood off them and blinked hard at the night sky, tears trickling down my face.

Get up. Yet every time I tried to move, pain exploded on the left side of my abdomen.

You can't lie here forever. You need to get up.

But I didn't have the strength. So instead, I closed my eyes and listened as a soft breeze whistled around me. I could no longer hear the train, and as much as I hoped to hear a voice nearby, all I heard was silence.

I imagined Star's figure emerging from the darkness. Maybe she'd call to me as she walked her way through the tall grass, a hand over her bloody belly.

Maybe...

I breathed in one last time and went to sleep again.

CHAPTER 36

I woke up to the sweet scent of lavender. The moment I opened my eyes, the pain returned, but I ignored it. Instead, I focused my thoughts on the floral scent.

Wincing, I sat upright.

Were my ribs broken? If so, I didn't know how many. I didn't know how to treat them, either. But I did recall reading something about shortness of breath being a dangerous sign. Fortunately, my breathing was fine.

With time, it would probably heal on its own.

It took everything in me to roll over onto my knees and make my way up to a standing position. Every time I tried to move my right arm, a blinding pain shot into my shoulder.

How was I supposed to get anywhere like this? Worse, where was I supposed to go? I squinted in the direction of the morning sun and toward the mountains standing tall beyond the horizon.

Maybe this was where I was meant to travel.

What are you doing, Silver?

I didn't have the answer. I had no clue what I was doing. The only skill set I had to survive the wild was my ability to harvest fruits and vegetables. Aside from that, I was useless. I couldn't fight, nor could I construct weapons. What good would it do me to grow potatoes if I didn't know how to start a fire or carve a knife?

You'll learn, I told myself. *You can do this.*

I wasn't sure if those thoughts were my own, or Grandma's. I liked to believe that Grandma was watching over me; it was the only comfort I could hold on to after learning of her death.

Grimacing with pain, I gripped the nearest tree for support. I wished I had a staff or something to help me walk, but for the time being, I would simply use the forest trees to get by.

I gazed up at the cliff from which I'd rolled down.

Although I couldn't see the train tracks from down here, I knew they continued east.

If I walked west, maybe I'd find Star, and then together, we could head east to find the others. It seemed like a reasonable plan, not that I had many options to choose from.

I moved through the forest one agonizing step at a time as birds chirped overhead, encouraging me to keep going. It was a beautiful sound that made me want to push onward.

I imagined what life might be like now for the people of Lutum. Had my speech encouraged them to return to work, or had they seen right through my lies? Would they attempt to take a stand against the Elites?

I shook these thoughts away. It didn't matter. I wasn't living in Lutum anymore, nor would I ever set foot there again; I was bound to a life of isolation on the outskirts. Dried brush and dead leaves crackled under my fancy white leather shoes as I moved. I wondered: what would a stranger think of me if they were to find me out here, in the wild? Would they mistake me for an Elite? I'd been forced to play dress-up before visiting the divisions. I hated these white clothes. I wanted to tear them apart and burn them.

"Star?" I called out.

My voice echoed for miles, frightening birds out of the trees and up into the sky.

No answer.

Every few steps, I shouted her name again. "Star!"

Nothing.

Was she dead? I hoped not. She'd been weaker than the rest of us with that cut across her belly. What if her fall had led to her wound reopening? To her bleeding out? I searched the forest, my head snapping from side to side.

Even if she didn't respond to my calls, it didn't mean she wasn't nearby. She could have easily been unconscious or in too much pain to shout. I walked in zigzags, searching through piles of leaves and inspecting the forest's dirt floor for prints. Farther ahead, beyond the forest, was a massive field of tall grass and wheat.

What if she'd rolled into the field?

I hurried along, making my way out of the forest when an eerie sound rumbled behind me.

At first, I thought maybe it was thunder, but the sky was clear.

It was a deep growling sound, followed by the snapping of branches.

I spun around. Behind me, three gray wolves walked slowly toward me with lowered heads and fierce yellow eyes. They were majestic with their silver coats, yet their large size made me want to run as fast as I could.

But if I ran, they would chase me. And ultimately, they'd catch me.

My breathing became shallow as my mind raced. I stared back, too afraid to break eye contact. If I let my guard down, I feared one of the wolves would lunge at me and tear my throat out.

The forest spun around me as I slowly walked backward. With every step I took, they took two.

The largest one moved the fastest, watching me with its ears folded back and its big wet nose sniffing the air.

This isn't real, my brain told me.

It couldn't be real. After everything I'd been through, I wasn't ready to die being torn apart by wolves.

My heart raced so fast that it was all I could focus on.

They were getting too close.

The large one snarled, its teeth snapping in the air, and I hopped backward a few steps.

I considered growling back but wasn't sure it would do anything. For all I knew, it would make things worse.

My throat, dry and sticky, made a clicking sound as I swallowed.

My heel caught something, and I stumbled backward. This seemed to excite the wolves. They drew in faster, preparing to lunge at me.

"Go!" I shouted. "Get!"

My voice carried through the forest, and the largest wolf bared its teeth at me, revealing bright red gums.

In a panic, I searched the forest floor for a stick, a rock... something. Anything.

If I couldn't run, I had to try to fight back.

I caught a glimpse of a sharp-edged stone about the size of my fist. It sat near the base of a tree, underneath a few yellow leaves.

Cautiously, I bent down and reached for the rock.

At once, all three wolves snarled at me, their wild eyes watching my every move. The large one bared its teeth again, countless folds appearing on its snout. It made it look like a vicious monster.

I froze midcrouch, my outstretched arm reaching for the rock. Maybe if I moved a bit slower...

Another snarl.

This time, the large wolf lunged forward and snapped its jaw in the air. I fell back, landing on my butt in a pile of leaves.

Behind him, the other wolves growled as they drew in, their shoulder bones poking through their fluffy coats.

It was now or never.

I threw myself at the rock, falling into leaves and branches, and stood up as quickly as I could when they came charging for me.

My sudden movement seemed to scare them.

I raised the rock above my head and

shouted as loud as I could. I managed to spook them a bit, but it wasn't enough to hold them off.

They were coming too close.

With all of my strength, I threw the rock straight at them.

All three wolves flinched as the rock smashed into leaves at their feet.

I'd missed. How could I have missed? It was over.

Without thinking, I darted in the opposite direction, running faster than my legs had ever carried me before. As I ran, rapid footsteps followed me through forest debris. To my surprise, I didn't feel any pain as I ran. I was so terrified that all I could think about was surviving—not dying.

A high-pitched whimper echoed from behind me and the footsteps stopped. Still running, I turned my head to the side to see what all the fuss was about, only to discover that the wolves had stopped chasing me.

The largest of the pack twirled in circles, trying to gnaw at the arrow sticking out of its bloody thigh. The other two scrambled with their ears flat on their heads as a dark figure approached.

The woman wore layers upon layers of clothing—skins, furs, and more. She marched forward without fear, and the wolves whimpered and ran away.

Once they disappeared, she set her bow behind her back and turned toward me.

As she drew in closer, I noticed fresh gashes across her face. They seemed to be a few days old and were now scabbing over. It looked like she'd been dragged across a rocky surface. Her skin, a light brown, matched her braided hair.

"Are you a Breeder?" she shouted.

How did she know about Breeders? About Olympus?

"I-I, um, yes," I stammered.

Her massive fur shoulder pads bounced as she approached me, squinting to get a good look at me.

"Another Breeder, so soon..." she mumbled.

Was she talking to me?

"Don't worry," she said, "I won't hurt you. Are you all right?"

The pain in my ribs and shoulder returned.

"I'm okay," I lied.

"You look injured," the woman said.

She had soft brown eyes, a noticeable overbite, and a protruding chin. She looked to be a few years older than me, maybe in her midtwenties. Although I couldn't see underneath the layers of mesh, vegetation, and animal hide, she seemed slim.

Her hair sat in a long messy braid that hung

over one shoulder.

"I realize this is a strange way to meet someone," she said, "but I promise you that you'll be taken someplace safe."

"Safe?" I asked. "Where?"

"We have a colony a few miles from here. You'll be treated for your injuries and nursed back to good health." She paused, then looked at my shoulder. "Is it dislocated?"

I tried to shrug and winced. "I-I don't know."

She moved toward me, and I thought of jumping back. But something told me I didn't have to be afraid of her. She was here to help me.

"Can I see?" she asked, reaching for my arm.

I froze as she moved in slow, assessing the damage. She dug her fingers into my shoulder and the pain made me cry out. "It's dislocated. I'll have to set it."

I wasn't sure what this meant. I wasn't even sure I understood what a dislocation was, but it sounded bad.

"Will it hurt?" I ask.

"It will," she said honestly. "But only for a second. I want you to count backward from ten."

"Ten," I said.

She yanked hard on my arm and something snapped. I cried out, my eyes wide.

"You okay?" she asked.

Was I okay? I'd never felt so much pain before. I rolled my shoulder back, and surprisingly, it felt okay.

"I-I think so," I said. "You mentioned a safe colony... What about my friends? I need to find—"

She smiled at me. "Don't worry. I know how the train works. We keep an eye on its movements at all times. We received word a few hours ago that the train was on the move and I was sent out to gather survivors."

"Survivors?" I asked.

Her smile faded. "Not everyone gets back up after they're tossed from the train. It all depends on where those bastards throw you."

I swallowed hard, thinking of Star, and the others who were no doubt tossed afterward.

"Your friends," she said. "Were any of them thrown off before you?"

I nodded fast. "Y-yeah. Star."

She lit up. "Don't you worry. Star's as stubborn as they come. If anyone would survive the fall, it's her."

"You know her?" I asked.

Her lips widened, and for the first time, I noticed hundreds of small, faded freckles across her nose and scarred, cratered cheek. When she caught me staring at the markings, she said, "Stone cliff. They threw me out face-first."

I winced.

"Come on," she said, grabbing her bow. "Let's go find Star."

We took a few steps toward the open field when she turned around and added, "What's your name, by the way?"

"Silver," I said. "Silverstasia Blackwood."

"Well, I'll be," she said as if she recognized my name. I didn't know this woman. How could she possibly know me?

"What?" I asked.

"Let's just say news travels fast," she said. She spun around, her body now facing me, and tilted her head. "I'm Penelope."

My jaw nearly fell to the ground.

Penelope.

She'd survived.

Maybe this meant I did stand a chance.

"People will be happy to meet you, Silver," she said. "You're exactly what our fighters need."

"Fighters?" I said, my head spinning.

She smirked knowingly at me. "For years, a colony has been forming outside of Olympus. We've been training fighters to take a stand against Olympus." She stared at me long enough to make me uncomfortable. "And now that you're here, I'd say that moment has come."

I wasn't sure what she meant, or what to make of it, but suddenly, I wondered if this was what Grandma had meant when she told me I'd accomplish great things in my life. Maybe with the help of Penelope and these *fighters* she spoke of, I could finally stand up to the Elites and their corruption.

I could fight back.

We could fight back.

Visit **shadeowens.com** for more works by Shade Owens, including book #2 of The Immortal Ones series.